Psycho Proctologists

Hakuna Matata, Vagina Dentata

by W.W. Pecker

Peckerhead Press

Psycho Proctologists – Hakuna Matata, Vagina Dentata

Peckerhead Press

Copyright 2013 by W.W. Pecker

Psycho Proctologists
Hakuna Matata, Vagina Dentata

The stripper drew a bead on me again and came over. This time she actually hopped off the stage, threw herself on my chair into my lap, and ground her nether goodies against the fabric of my jeans. At the same time, she wrapped her arms around my neck, thrust her boobies in my face again.

"Well?" she prompted. "Where's the demon?"

"I—I—" *Shit!* Ever since she'd taken the stage, the only demon I could concentrate on was the one in my pants. I'd totally neglected my mission. Some undercover operative I was turning out to be.

I was spared an answer by the sudden sound of screaming. It took a moment for it to register over the blare of the music, but it was unmistakably a series of shrill, high-pitched shrieks of terror—and very likely pain . . .

Psycho Proctologists

Published by Peckerhead Press

*This book is sanctimoniously dedicated to
One Million Moms*

*Stalwart guardians of decency and morality,
scourge of the debased and the depraved
whether you like it or not, bitches!*

CHAPTER ONE

Jerry McTitties' Gentlemen's Club—*Live Girls!*—reeked of demons.

Okay, it didn't really *smell* like demons. That's a bit of a misstatement. I don't literally have a nose for demons, but I do have an eye for them. A third eye.

No, not that kind of third eye.

"Christ, Mikey!" Fister, in the driver's seat of his brown Ford probe, said as we sat in the parking lot. "You're glowing like a traffic light. We must be close."

I nodded across the parking lot at the strip joint. "It's in there. I can tell."

"Well, what are we waiting for?" Fister and I both turned around and regarded our tagalong in the back seat. Henry, our thirteen-year-old charge for the evening, sat in his customary honey badger outfit that looked like a cross between a bad pair of pajamas and a costume for a school play. "Let's go kick its ass."

"Not so fast there, kemosabe," I said. "It's already past your bedtime on a school night. Your mother would kill the both of us if she knew we had you out chasing a demon."

Henry rolled his eyes. "Whatevs. You wouldn't even have found it if it weren't for me."

That much was true. Henry—or Morpheus, in his online persona—had gotten a tip only a few hours ago from one of his contacts that there was a demon of unspecified type hanging around in this neighborhood, one of the seediest in Compton. To be honest, I wasn't sure what frightened me more: being this close to a demon of unknown variety, or hanging around after dark in Compton.

"It doesn't matter," I said. "Your mother gave us express instructions to have you in bed by nine thirty with your homework done."

Henry shrugged. "What she doesn't know won't hurt her. It's not like I'm going to tell her. Relax, will ya? As uptight as you are, your spinal cord would fall out your asshole if you unclenched just for a second."

"But . . . this could be dangerous."

"We've taken out demons before," Henry pointed out. "No worries."

"Yeah, Mikey," Fister said. "No worries. Hakuna matata."

I rolled my eyes. "You've been getting stoned and watching *The Lion King* again, haven't you? You know you shouldn't—"

I was derailed in mid-sermon by the sudden interruption of Gloria Gaynor. I frowned, confused, until I realized that it was Henry's cell phone. What kind of a thirteen-year-old kid used "I Will Survive" as a ringtone?

Henry checked the call on his cell phone screen and flashed me a grin. "Speak of the devil," he said.

"What?" I cried, suddenly panicked. "Is that . . . that's your mother? *Shit!*"

"Relax," Fister told me. "She's all the way across the country. She'll never know we're not at your place."

"Are you insane?" I cried. "You know her. She just . . . knows things."

"Would you two mind shutting the fuck up for a second?" Henry said. "I gotta take this." Fister and I both shot each other a panicked look, then closed our mouths in unison. We swiveled our heads around to focus on Henry in the back seat, waiting with held breath to hear if Victoria would lose her shit on us when she got back from Boca Raton.

"Hi, mom!" Henry said. "How's the twat fest?" He grinned and gave Fister and me a thumbs-up sign while he listened to his mother's reply. "Yeah, yeah, mom, I know it's a gynecologists' convention—I mean, conference—I was just fucking with you." I couldn't quite hear Victoria's words, since Henry had the phone up to his ear, but I could make out the tone well enough, and my imagination could fill in well enough what Victoria had likely said: *Henry! Language!*

My suspicions were confirmed a second later as Henry continued: "Sorry, mom. Yeah. I'm fine." Pause. "Just . . . doing my Spanish homework. Mikey's been helping me. He's really good at Spanish. You know—conjugating verbs and shit—oops, I mean stuff. You know—*tú chupas vergas grandes, ella chupa mi verga grande, todas las putas chupan vergas grandes. . .*"

My jaw dropped open. "I—I did not teach him that!" I protested, hopefully loudly enough so that Victoria would hear me through the connection.

Henry covered the phone with his hand and held up a hand to forestall any further protests. "Relax," he whispered to me. "She never took a lick of Spanish. She sucks at languages. She only managed to pass French in college 'cause she took a lick of her professor."

I tried to ignore Fister's salacious leer as Henry put the phone back up to his ear. "Yeah, mom. Uh-huh. Sure. You know I will. Of course. Okay, no problem. Love you, too. Bye." But instead of hanging up, he held the phone out to me. "She wants to talk to you."

I glanced over at Fister. "Me?" I gulped.

"Well, go on," Fister said.

Resignedly, I took the phone from Henry and put it up to my ear. "Hello?" I said, and I hated how my voice cracked. "Oh, hi, Victoria! Nice to hear from you."

"Are you at home?" Victoria asked me immediately.

I grimaced at Henry. I was a terrible liar—and Victoria knew it. Without a doubt, that's why she'd asked to speak to me, and not to Fister. Henry spread his hands helplessly and gave me an exasperated *come on, say something* gesture.

"Um—of course. We are. We definitely are. Why wouldn't we be?" I said.

"You're lying," Victoria's voice said.

Panicked, I took the cell phone away from my mouth and covered the speaker with my hand. "She knows," I whispered to Henry. "What do I do?"

"Just . . . fuck, make something up," Henry said.

I glared at him. Why did he get me into these messes? First, convincing me to come all the way out to Buttfuck Compton after dark, and then lying to his mother . . .

With a sigh, I put the phone back up to my ear. "I—I'm not lying," I said. "I just . . . I didn't . . . oh, hell, I admit it! I let Henry watch Animal Planet. I know you told me not to . . . I'm so sorry! You were right, he totally gets off on it. I'm sorry I didn't believe you. I had to make a special trip to the grocery store last night to buy extra Kleenex. God, I can't believe how much he whacks off."

There was a golden moment of silence from everyone—Victoria, Fister, and even Henry, who sat staring at me, mortified.

Then, finally, Victoria said: "It's all right. Just . . . be more careful, okay?"

"I will. You bet."

"I gotta go. Talk to you later. Tell Henry 'bye for me, and that I love him."

"Will do. Have fun at your conference."

"'Bye."

"'Bye."

I hung up the phone and tossed it back to Henry. He caught it. Finally, he managed to master his voice, and said: "Dude. That was totally fucked up."

"It worked, didn't it? Would you rather I told her we're sitting outside a strip joint in the seediest neighborhood known to man? Now how about we all figure out a way to flush out this demon?"

"Sometimes, I really hate you guys," I muttered as I headed across the parking lot toward the main entrance to Jerry McTitties'.

"Hey, you lost the rock-paper-scissors war," Fister said into the invisible Bluetooth earpiece I was wearing that connected me to him from the car. Since we'd agreed to team up with Victoria for the purpose of demon hunting, we'd gone all high-tech. EBay's a wonderful thing. "Besides, somebody's gotta stay in the car with the kid."

"I'd have gone in myself," Henry's sometimes husky, sometimes reedy adolescent voice said over our connection, "but I don't think I'd have gotten past the bouncer."

He had a point there.

"Besides," Fister continued, "you need some boobies in your life, Mikey. Real in-your-face ones, not ones on a computer screen."

Fister had a point there, too. Though if I'd been able to relax, I might have enjoyed my undercover assignment a bit more. As it was, following the divining rod of my second sight toward a demon inside the club, my heart was thumping a spasmodic patter-patter beat inside my chest.

Inside the front door, I paid the twenty dollar cover charge to a man smoking a cigarette behind a glass window. He took my bill, then looked up at me expectantly. I fidgeted for a second. What was the routine here? The last time I'd been to a strip club had been on my twenty-first birthday, as a pre-med student.

"ID?" he prompted.

"Oh. Of course." I fished in my wallet and extricated my driver's license. I slid it through the opening in the glass window.

He took it, examined it, took a puff of his cigarette, then slid my license back to me. "Nice shades," he muttered.

"Thank you." I hesitated. *They're Oakley*, I would have added, but thankfully he gestured me on with a flick of his thumb before I could utter any inanity. Relieved, I headed around a black velvet-draped partition, following the thumping blare of bass-drenched music.

"I'm in," I said to Fister and Henry.

"In what?" Henry said, and snickered. So did Fister.

Christ. As if babysitting one thirteen-year-old weren't bad enough without Fister's adolescent humor.

I stood for a moment surveying the interior of the club. Four slightly raised stage islands fitted with poles dotted the room, the patrons seated around each enjoying the busts on display in a pick-your-poison kind of arrangement. The nearest island to me boasted a slim brunette with pointy nipples and a G-string that looked like a sliver of dental floss up her ass. Farther back and to the left, the next island was staffed by a busty blonde, then on the right side of the club a curvaceous redhead, and finally, on the lip of the island in the farthest corner, near the DJ booth, an African-American beauty who could have been a gymnast, judging by how she was sitting on her ass and grabbing her ankles up in the air with her legs scissored open while a flannelled redneck with a five-dollar bill in his teeth leaned in close enough to breathe into her crotch.   All the while, a half-dozen bikini-clad waitresses weaved among the various islands carrying trays of drinks, and another trio of topless floor girls spaced strategically along the floor gave lap dances to various seated gentlemen.

"I told you we should have sprung for the video sunglasses," Henry's voice said in my ear. He was talking to Fister, but even so I had to bite my tongue to keep from responding. It would not do to be seen muttering to myself here inside the club. I didn't want to draw the attention of the muscly bouncer dressed in a black tank-top standing unobtrusively over in the back corner by the DJ booth.

I opted for the third island, where the redhead was busy squeezing a wad of dollar-bills between her tits, teasing her audience of roughly a dozen young men—who might have been in a bachelor party—to see if they could fit another one into her cleavage.   I surreptitiously plunked down into a chair next to the stage and watched the redhead, my eyes focused on the lucky wad of cash and her rosy areolae—

I mentally kicked myself. I was here to find a demon, not enjoy the spectacle of fleshy mounds of delight sprinkled with just a touch of silver glitter—

Focus, I told myself, wrenching my gaze away from the redhead's jigglies. I'd always had a thing for redheads. Instead, I surveyed the rest of the club, looking for telltale signs of demon possession. It was hard, because usually the tells were in the eyes: completely blackened eyes where the whites had completely disappeared, or glowing red pupils, or sometimes yellow eyes—but none of the patrons in the club, for obvious reasons, made it easy for me to stare into their eyes.

The music came to an end, and we hit the changeover. The redhead nimbly collected all the cash strewn on her stage into a cowboy hat and withdrew, to be replaced only an instant later with another redhead. I took a break from my reconnaissance of the joint for a split second to spare the new girl a glance—

"Oh, fuck me," I muttered: it was Victoria.

"Ooh, Mikey, behave yourself," Fister's voice said in my ear. "You devil you."

"Dayum!" I heard Henry's voice in the background. "Is he getting a lap dance already? Doesn't mess around, does he?"

"No!" I protested. "It's . . . it's not like that." And then I realized that I'd completely forgotten my own rule of not looking like a crazy man talking to myself. Nothing would attract the attention of the bouncer faster. But with Henry and Fister in my ear and Victoria in my sight and the proximity of a demon setting off my Spidey sense, I was beginning to experience an odd sort of perception-fuck. I needed way more practice separating the input from my various senses.

There wasn't time, however. As Victoria got up onto the stage and grasped the pole, she caught sight of me slinking down in my chair and shot me a look that might have looked seductive to any casual observer, but knowing Victoria—and when we'd met she'd held a knife to my throat and threatened to kill me—I knew it to be more like a *what the fuck, mister?* look. I'd just told her not ten minutes ago on the phone that I was safe and sound in my condo with her son doing his homework at my kitchen table.

Of course, all things being equal, she had told me a bit of a white lie, as well. She was supposed to be all the way across the country in Boca at a gynecologist's convention, not dressed in a naughty nurse's outfit, complete with a plunging neckline, a skirt that would have been illegal in several countries, and a real stethoscope, ready to twine her twat around a stripper pole—and make an entire bachelor party's worth of horny young men very happy. She could totally rock the MILF vibe, that much was certain.

Jerry McTitties' DJ had the changeover down to a science. After only the briefest break in the music, the *thumpa thumpa* beat began again, and the ladies manning the poles on the four islands across the floor began their routines. Victoria began hers by humping the pole with rhythmic pelvic thrusts, then strutting to the lip of the stage and teasing her own private little audience by clutching her boobs. And she really was a pro: the bachelor party was riveted, and I—

—*Focus*, a dim part of my brain reminded me. *You're here to flush out a demon, not—*

My thought derailed completely as Victoria fixed her gaze on me in the audience. She gave me a sultry beckon with her index finger. I gulped. She strutted over to me, her hips—and *fuck me*, what a pair of hips—sashaying to the music, and on the way she ripped off the faux leather belt that held her nurse's one-piece costume closed. The folds hung open, revealing a maddening slice of lingerie-lined breasts below.

She was in front of me in an instant. She used the belt as a makeshift lasso, threw it around my neck, and drew my face in close—so very, very close—to her boobs. Our heads were so close, close enough for me to reach out and lick her neck. As a reflex, I licked the tip of my tongue—

"If you're here for the same reason I am, then you'd better play the part, motherfucker," she breathed in my ear—the one with the receiver in it. "When I come back, you'd better have a twenty-dollar bill between your teeth."

And just like that, she ditched me there. She retreated back onto stage, did a few token gymnastics on the pole, and then maneuvered over to pay some special attention to the gentlemen of the bachelor party.

Fister and Henry chortled in my ear. Given the eerie similarity of their chortles, they might have been father and son. "Well go on, Mikey," Fister hooted, "don't be a cheap bastard. You heard the lady. You'd better treat her right."

"Yeah, Mikey," Henry echoed. "Don't be cheap. She sounds way hot."

Ew, I thought. *You wouldn't say that if you knew she was your mother.* Nevertheless, Victoria had given me a directive. I bent over and fumbled my wallet out of my pocket with trembling fingers. I opened it and squinted in the dim light of the club—

Fuck. No twenties. Only ones, a five, and a fifty. I plucked it out of my wallet and stuck it between my teeth, just as Victoria had directed—

—just in time to see her jiggle her way back over to my side of the stage. In the time it had taken me to pull the money out of my wallet, she'd lost the top to her naughty nurse's outfit. Now the only thing covering her mounds was a lacy white bra that caused an instant case of blue balls for the brain.

She drew a bead on me again and came over. This time she actually hopped off the stage, threw herself on my chair into my lap, and ground her nether goodies against the fabric of my jeans. At the same time, she wrapped her arms around my neck, thrust her boobies in my face again.

"Well?" she prompted. "Where's the demon?"

"I—I—" *Shit!* Ever since she'd taken the stage, the only demon I could concentrate on was the one in my pants. I'd totally neglected my mission. Some undercover operative I was turning out to be.

I was spared an answer by the sudden sound of screaming. It took a moment for it to register over the blare of the music, but it was unmistakably a series of shrill, high-pitched shrieks of terror—and very likely pain.

Everybody in the club had heard it, apparently. A moment later the DJ cut the music . . . and there it was again: a full-lunged peal of terror if ever there was one.

Victoria climbed off my lap and cocked her head to listen. Everyone in the club was looking around, confused and more than a little nervous in the sudden silence.

"This way," Victoria said. And without waiting to see if I'd follow her, she bolted off toward the back end of the club.

I stood and followed after Victoria, pausing only long enough to adjust myself inside my pants so I didn't sprain something while running. Victoria led me to a back section of the club, down a curtained-off back corridor that housed a trio of private rooms—most likely for the high dollar customers that wanted a private show with a few more frills.

"Mikey, what's going on?" Fister's voice asked. "Mikey, talk to me!"

"Stay tuned," I told him.

Victoria flung open the first door. It was unlocked; the room was empty. Undaunted, Victoria tried the next one. This one was locked, so she drew back and kicked it in, heedless of her fuck-me heels. This room was occupied by a fat man who was fumbling with his pants while one of the establishment's ladies was struggling back into a bikini top. They yelped in fright at Victoria's entrance, but their yelps were the ordinary kind of those caught in a compromising position; I could discern nothing out of the ordinary about them—certainly nothing to account for those soul-rending screams.

"Mikey?" Fister called. "Fuck, Mikey, report! What's going on? Christ. We're coming in for backup."

"Negative," I said, but I feared I was too late. The sound of a car door opening sounded clearly through the audio implant.

Victoria moved to door number three. She poised to kick it in, but then reconsidered and jiggled the handle. It swung open.

Inside, in the dim halogen lights, a man sat on the couch along one wall. He was alone, as far as I could tell; the room was barely more than a cubicle, so there didn't seem to be anywhere for fearsome demons to hide, but I'd been in the demon hunting business just long enough to take nothing for granted. I automatically checked the ceiling for any potential droppy-slitheries as Victoria rushed over to the man.

I saw why as she plunked down on the couch next to him. He was clutching his right hand and grimacing in pain. I squinted in the dim light, and saw that the tip of his right middle finger was missing—and bleeding like a motherfucker.

Victoria was immediately in charge. "Bob!" she called. She snapped her fingers in front of the man's face, and when that failed to focus his pain-filled abstraction, she slapped him. "Bob!" She said again. "Look at me!"

I frowned. "You know this guy?"

"Of course. He's a regular." Victoria snapped her fingers one more time in front of Bob's eyes, and he finally managed to focus on her. "Easy, Bob," Victoria said. "You're going to be all right. Don't worry. I'm a doctor."

Bob took a couple of half-sobs, half-breaths, and frowned. "You—you're a doctor? What the hell are you doing working here?"

"Never mind that now." Victoria cast about in vain for something to use to apply pressure to his wound. Finding nothing else handy, she shimmied out of her skirt, leaving her clad only in a pair of lacy panties that matched her bra. Then, she ripped a strip off the skirt and applied it to the stump of the man's finger. He sucked in a breath and flinched in pain, but didn't cry out. "Hold this," she instructed Bob. "Don't worry. An ambulance is on the way." Victoria looked across the room at me. "Isn't it?"

I frowned. "I . . . don't know."

"Christ, that was a hint, Mikey. Call an ambulance already, will ya?"

"Oh. Right."

I fished my iPhone out of my front pocket and fiddled with dialing while Victoria took Bob's left hand and gently helped him to apply pressure to the wound. "Everything's going to be all right, Bob," Victoria soothed. "I know it hurts, but it's not life-threatening. People lose fingers all the time."

Not in strippers, I thought.

"I need you to talk to me," Victoria said to Bob. "Who did this to you?"

Bob looked at her like a child with a boo-boo, but her manner was getting through to him. Damn, she was a hell of a physician. She was wasting her calling as a gynecologist. "Ch—Cherry," he stammered.

"Cherry? You're sure?"

Bob nodded.

"Where did she go?"

Bob indicated the door. "She left."

Victoria looked to me. "Then she can't have gone far. We've gotta go after her." She turned back to Bob. "I've gotta go now, Bob. But I want you to keep applying pressure to your finger, you hear? Help'll be here before you know it."

Victoria stood up. She turned to me—

—and at that moment, Fister and Henry barreled to a halt right behind me in the doorframe. "What happened?" Fister demanded, out of breath.

I turned to gape at him. "How the hell did you two get past the bouncer?"

Fister shrugged. "I just shouted 'LAPD!' and kept going. The bouncer was smoking a doobie, so he didn't protest."

Victoria registered the new arrivals, and then fixed me with her trademark glare that left tread marks all over my soul. "You brought my son to a strip joint?"

"Victoria?" Fister said, confused. "I don't understand—what are you doing—?" His gaze was immediately drawn to Victoria's rack. "It's . . . nice to see you."

Fister wasn't the only one surprised to see her. "Mom?" Henry said.   Henry stood in the doorframe, blinking stupidly. "Mom . . . oh my god, put some clothes on!"

I looked from Victoria, to Henry, to Fister. "That's gonna need some therapy," I muttered.

"Well," Victoria said, "at least the gang's all here. Come on, boys. We've got some work to do." She paused just long enough to look back over her shoulder at Bob. "Let that be a lesson to you," she said. "Never finger the strippers." Then, she pushed past me, Fister, and Henry and back into the club proper. "My car's parked out back. Come on. We've gotta find Cherry."

CHAPTER TWO

Victoria led us down the back hallway of Jerry McTitties' Gentlemen's Club, where she unceremoniously pushed in a black-painted door— the dressing room for the club's performers, I gathered. It was mostly empty, save for a pair of brunettes. One of them stood clad only in lace panties, and the other was marginally more clothed, with one tasseled pasty on and one off. "Victoria?" this one said as Victoria charged through. "What's going on? We heard—" She caught sight of Fister, me, and Henry trailing behind, and yipped in surprise. She covered her breasts with her hands. A fine time for modesty, I thought.

Victoria retrieved her purse from between a pair of leather panties on a table in the corner. "Everything's fine," she said. "Did Cherry go through this way?"

The pastied brunette nodded. "Just a minute or so ago. She looked like she was in a hurry. She's not in trouble, is she?"

"No time to explain," Victoria said. She fished her car keys out of her purse and tossed them to Fister. "You'd better drive," she said. "I'm not really dressed for it." She grabbed a black leather trench coat off a costume rack next to the table, then followed it with a black felt hat that completed the ensemble and made her look like something straight out of *The Maltese Falcon*—a stripperized version of a private dick. "Come on."

Fister followed her, and I followed behind him. I made it only a pair of steps before I realized Henry wasn't trotting along behind me as I'd thought. I turned, and saw that he was flashing the two ladies a rakish, dumbass grin. "Henry!" I bellowed. "No time for gawking."

But Henry didn't move. He plucked a string thong off of the table. "Were these Cherry's?" he asked.

The pastied brunette nodded.

"Mind if I borrow these?"

"Aw," the other girl said. "Aren't you cute?"

I crossed back to him, grabbed his wrist, and hauled him with me. He brought Cherry's underwear in tow.

The dressing room had a service exit that opened out onto the club's private back parking lot. It was a prime place for the ladies' cigarette breaks, I judged by the littered cigarette butts all over the concrete.

Victoria stopped about halfway across the little parking lot. "She must have gone on foot," she said. "Her Lexus is still here."

"Cherry drives a Lexus?" I said. "What kind of a stripper drives a Lexus?"

"She's got a fan base," Victoria said. "What can I say? She gives head in the private booths, and most of the customers know it."

We piled into Victoria's Azera—Fister in the driver's seat, Victoria into the passenger seat, and Henry and me in the back seat. Henry and I were barely strapped in when Fister threw the car into gear and throttled out of the parking lot, which angled down a narrow dirt alley around the side of Jerry McTitties' before dumping us out onto the main road.

"Which way?" Fister asked.

"Turn left," Victoria instructed.

Fister did, and we were soon rocketing down a seedy street in Compton, keeping our eyes peeled for Cherry.

"So," Fister said, grinning, his eyes flicking over to Victoria, sneaking a peek at the outline of her lacy bra that was just visible in the tented opening of the trench coat, "how's the gynecologists' convention?"

"Very funny," Victoria said. She shook her head in disgust. "I worked that club four nights in a row trying to flush out the demon. I almost had it before you two douchewads showed up and fucked it all up."

"What?" Fister said. "You mean it took you four nights to figure out it was Cherry? Shit, Bob fingered her a lot easier than you did." He chuckled at his own joke.

"It's not like a regular demon possession," Victoria said defensively. "This one's different. There are none of the obvious tells."

"She's right," I said. My Spidey sense that divined demons had been utterly confused in the club. It'd sensed that there was a demon nearby, but other than that, it'd been utterly useless. "This one's different."

"Let me guess," Henry cut into the conversation, leaning forward in the back seat. "It was hiding in her snatch?"

"Henry!" Victoria said. "Don't be vulgar."

"Sorry, mom," Henry said.

"Wait a minute." Victoria turned around in the passenger seat to regard her son. "We'll have the conversation later about what you're doing at a strip joint on a school night, young man, but for the moment . . . how did you know to come here?"

"We got a tip," Henry said. "Or rather, Morpheus did."

"So did Cherry," Fister put in.

Victoria withered Fister to silence with a glare, then turned back to Henry. "A tip from whom? Which one of your contacts?"

Henry scrunched up his brow in concentration. "Um—it was Mutton Jeff, I think." He shook his head. "Or was it MuffMuncher Jeff? I can't quite remember. I get those two confused. Why? Who tipped you off?"

"It doesn't matter," Victoria said.

"Of course it matters," Henry said. "Who was it?"

"A . . . friend."

"What kind of friend convinces you to go undercover as a stripper?"

"Well," Victoria said, "actually, the stripping was my idea." A pregnant silence hung in the car. Henry and I both raised our eyebrows at Victoria. Even Fister took his eyes off the road and looked questioningly over at her. "What?" Victoria demanded. "I'm a grown woman. It was . . . nice. To know I've still got it. Ya know?"

Don't worry, I thought. I still couldn't get her hip thrusts and gyrations and pole ministrations out of my mind. *You've definitely still got it.*

"I get it," Fister said. "A nice trip down mammary lane."

I groaned. "God, Fisty, just drive, will ya?"

A brief moment of silence reigned inside the vehicle. Then: "I don't get it," Henry said.

"It's . . . don't worry about it, champ," I said. "It wasn't really that funny."

"No, not that," Henry said, annoyed. "I mean, I don't get why Cherry would leave her vehicle in the parking lot and head off on foot. There's nothing really out here. We'd have seen her by now, unless—"

I followed Henry's line of logic perfectly. "Unless she had an accomplice," I finished his thought for him. "Somebody must have picked her up."

"Fuck!" Victoria swore. "If that's true, she could be anywhere by now."

"She still can't have gotten that far," Fister pointed out. "All we gotta do is look in cars for hot broads—"

"In Compton?" Victoria said. "That's like looking for a needle in a haystack. They don't call this the Hooker Highway for nothing."

"Really?" Fister frowned. "Hooker highway? Here? I always go over to—"

"She could have gotten in any vehicle, and we'd never know it." Victoria pounded her fist on the passenger side dashboard. "Godfuckingdammit! So close, only to lose her now."

I didn't know what to say. Neither did Fister or Henry, apparently—for once. A long, uncomfortable, frustrated silence lingered inside the vehicle. Finally, Fister said, "How about pancakes?"

Victoria looked at him. "What?"

"How about pancakes?" Fister repeated. "There's a Denny's just up ahead."

Victoria narrowed her eyes. "There's a demon running around on the loose, and you want pancakes?"

"You got a better idea?" Fister said. "We could drive around here for hours and not find her—I mean 'it.' I'm hungry." And without waiting for a consensus, Fister pulled Victoria's Azera into the Denny's parking lot.

We surely made an odd quartet as we made our entrance into the Denny's: Victoria dressed in a long black trench coat and detective hat, Henry in his honey badger outfit, Fister wearing a blue and orange Hawaiian shirt that looked like a garish sunset, and then me, wearing my Oakleys indoors at night. Otherwise, I was the only one even remotely tastefully dressed, in my Dockers khakis and polo shirt. To her credit, though, the waitress who seated us didn't even raise an eyebrow at our oddness. "Aw, aren't you cute?" she said to Henry.

Henry flashed her his nascent lothario grin. "So I'm told," he said.

We settled into a booth. Fister sat next to Victoria, and I sat on the inside next to Henry. And as soon as I was seated, I realized I was indeed hungry. Demon hunting was hard work.

We all ordered. I opted for a blueberry waffle, Fister the banana nut pancakes, and Henry a super slam breakfast. I raised an eyebrow at the sheer amount of food, but then, he was thirteen, I reminded myself. But Victoria surprised me a moment later by ordering the same, with an extra side of bacon. She handed the menu back to the waitress, who headed back toward the kitchen to put in our orders. Only then did Victoria look back to Fister and to me, who were both staring at her, wondering where she planned to put all the food. Her eyes narrowed. "First person who says anything loses a finger," she said.

Fister and I immediately put on our best innocent expressions. "You mean like Bob?" Fister said.

"What?" I said. "I don't—"

I leaned forward over the table before Victoria could scowl him to death. "So," I said to Victoria, "how about you tell us what you know about this demon you've been hunting for the last four days?" *And why you didn't tell us about it*, I hoped she grasped in my subtext. *I thought we were a team.*

For the first time since I'd met her, Victoria looked uncomfortable. She glanced self-consciously at Henry, who missed it, as he was slamming his glass of Dr. Pepper. "Not much more than you do, unfortunately," she said. "I didn't know much about the demon until tonight." She stared down at the table.

She was a shitty liar, but I sensed that whatever she was reluctant to reveal had something to do with Henry. "So," I said, "what is it we're dealing with, then? It's not a run-of-the-mill possession, I'll warrant."

Victoria shook her head. "No. I don't think it's anything like that. You should have been able to sense that."

I'd thought as much. "And I'm guessing it's not a fully incarnated demon, either. Otherwise Cherry would've . . ."

"She'd have popped," Fister put in. Henry snorted Dr. Pepper, and Fister grinned like an idiotic schoolboy, pleased with his joke. They shared a fist bump. They really were kindred souls. Victoria and I made eye contact and simultaneously rolled our eyes.

"I think it must be some kind of demonic parasite," Victoria said. "Some kind of hybrid from the demon realm, but spawned in ours."

I looked to Henry. "Are you familiar with anything like that?" I asked.

He shrugged. "Sure. I've got documentation on at least a dozen different varieties of demon hybrids. But I've never heard of any that incubate in women's snatches."

"It's a prime place," Fister mused. "It's warm, moist . . ."

"What do you know about Cherry?" I asked. "Why her? Why would a demon hybrid choose her? You'd think if a demon hybrid were incubating in her . . . ahm . . . private parts . . . a stripper wouldn't be the most logical choice. Especially Cherry. I mean, she practically flashes her . . . um . . . you know—"

"Mikey, you're a doctor, for Christ's sake," Fister cut in. "Will you just say it already? Her *vagina*!"

Immediately, all the conversations in the restaurant ceased. The eyes of all the other patrons at all the other tables were on us. I felt my face light on fire. A middle-aged couple was undisguisedly scowling at us. I coughed and hunched down in the booth and took a long, long sip of my Diet Coke.

Excruciatingly slowly, the conversations around the restaurant resumed. This time, Fister leaned in close over the table and said in a voice barely above a whisper, "Maybe somebody wanted Bob to stick a finger in Cherry."

"You think Bob was a target?" I asked. It was a distinct possibility. Bob apparently had enough money to spend multiple nights a week at Jerry McTitties' and tip strippers into the private rooms in the back . . .

"It's a place to start," Fister said. "What do you know about Bob?"

"Not much," Victoria said. "He drives an oil tanker. He seemed harmless. Always had plenty of money to spend on the girls, but didn't exactly seem like the type to have demon-conjurers for enemies."

"He never asked you to go back into one of the private rooms?"

"What?"

"Did he ever try to finger you?"

"What? No!"

"Just asking."

"What about a lap dance? Did he ever ask you for a lap dance?"

"No."

"Put any money in your G-string?"

"What does that have to do with anything?"

Fister shrugged. "Just asking."

Henry stood up immediately. For the first time since I'd met the kid, he looked a little uncomfortable. "I—uh—I'm gonna take a piss," he said. "Excuse me." He high-tailed it toward the front end of the restaurant—quite literally. The tail on his honey badger costume bobbed in his haste.

Fister frowned. "What's up with him? Is he feeling all right—?"

I shook my head. Sometimes, Fister could be so dense. "You'd beat it, too, if someone gave you the mental image of someone sticking dollar bills in your mother's G-string."

Fister blinked at me, nonplussed. Inwardly, I counted to three as he visibly processed my statement, and right on cue, the mental image of his mother in a G-string struck home. He succumbed to a face-contorting grimace. And then, when that had run its course, he looked at Victoria and said in an uncharacteristically subdued voice: "Oh."

With Henry in the bathroom, I decided to seize my opportunity. I leaned forward and fixed Victoria with my best clinical gaze, the one I used with patients who tried to bullshit me. "So what is it?" I asked. "What is it you're not telling us?"

Victoria feigned indignance first. "What—?" she sputtered. But then, she abandoned the pretense with a big sigh. "All right," she said. "But you've got to promise not to tell Henry."

Fister and I looked to each other, then back to her. "All right," we said in unison.

"I—I think I've seen this kind of demon before."

"Where?" I asked.

"College. More than fifteen years ago now. I think this is the same kind of demon who killed Henry's father."

She never talked about Henry's father. "I didn't realize he was dead," I said. "I'm sorry."

She took a moment to compose herself, and then continued. "I guess everyone does some things in college they're not too proud of."

"You mean like stripping?"

"No," she said. "Not that. I was a hell of a stripper."

Still are, I thought. "Go on," I said.

"The club I worked for . . . one night we got a gig for an off-site at Henry's father's frat house. I was scheduled to go, but I traded my shift with one of the other girls."

"Because you didn't want all of Henry's father's frat brothers pawing you?" I said. "I can imagine—" *how awkward that would be,* I was going to say, but Victoria cut me off.

"No, nothing like that," she said. "I'd just found out I was pregnant with Henry, and I hadn't told his father yet. I wasn't sure I was going to tell him, either. I thought about . . . about not having Henry."

"I see."

"So anyway, one of the other girls—Maggie, her name was—went to the frat house off-site in my place. The next morning the police found every member of the frat . . . dead. You can imagine how."

I connected the dots in my head. Fister must have, too, because we both cringed at the same time. We both fidgeted, uncomfortable. When I managed to overcome my serious case of the willies, I said, "That's . . . I'm so sorry."

Victoria stared down at the table, and traced figure eights with her index finger in the ring of condensation from her soft drink. "I should have gone," she said, her voice choked. "I should have gone. If I had, he'd still be alive."

"You couldn't have known," I said. "It wasn't your fault."

"What about Maggie?" Fister cut in. "What happened to her?"

Victoria shrugged. "Who knows? She just disappeared. The police looked all over for her, but she'd skipped town. Or skipped the country. She hasn't been seen since, to my knowledge. And believe me, I've spent the last fifteen years looking."

"So . . . when you got word of this demon at Jerry McTitties', you thought it might be the same demon that killed your . . . um . . . your—" I couldn't find the right word. I had no idea what Victoria and Henry's father had been to each other. *Husband* wasn't right . . . *lover*, maybe? *Baby daddy* was probably the most accurate, but didn't exactly sound the most compassionate.

"Uh-huh," Victoria said. "The MO was the same."

"So who tipped you off?" I asked. "How did you find out? It wasn't one of Henry's—Morpheus's—contacts, surely?" I did the math in my head. Victoria must have gotten the tipoff at least three days before Henry's extensive web of online demon hunters had managed to get the alert to him.

"No. It was an anonymous email."

I groaned. "You went undercover hunting a demon at a strip joint based on an anonymous contact? Are you crazy? Did you ever happen to think it could have been a trap?"

Victoria shrugged. "I can handle myself."

Well, that much was certainly true. The first time I'd met her, she'd practically sliced out my jugular with a knife. "That's not the point. You should have told us."

Victoria withered me with a glare. "So you could take my son to a strip joint, you mean?"

"Well . . . I mean . . . *no*!" I fumbled for words. "Fister and I could've helped. You didn't have to alert Henry."

"No offense, but the two of you are totally shitty liars. You'd have never managed to keep a secret from Henry."

"I—" A protest died on my lips. "All right, fair enough," I admitted finally. "But what do we do now? We're all on the case now—even Henry. You're stuck with us."

"Well, one of you two could start by checking the bathroom. Henry's been in there for an awful long time."

She was right. I hadn't noticed in my preoccupation with Victoria's story, but Henry had been gone for quite some time. Of course, in the last four nights he'd spent at my house, he'd locked himself in the bathroom for long periods of time, but that was only to be expected from a thirteen-year-old. "I'll go," I said.

I got up from the table and headed back toward the men's bathroom at the back of the restaurant. It was in a recessed alcove that gave me eerie flashbacks to the private rooms at the back of Jerry McTitties'. Fortunately, this was better lit.

"Henry?" I called, pushing open the door. "Henry, are you—"

I stopped. Henry was indeed inside. I should have been relieved—except he was on his knees in front of the first of a pair of urinals, with his face stuck inside the porcelain trough, licking the urinal cake.

"Henry?" I said, utterly dumbfucked. "Henry . . .? Geez, Henry, what the *fuuuuuck*?"

He didn't answer. Instead, he swiveled his head around to look at me, a scowl of rage on his face.

I instinctively took a step back. And then I noticed that his eyes were a deep shade of yellow, the telltale sign of a demon possession.

I stood there, locked in stupefied indecision, torn between running and screaming like a total pussy. Fortunately, before I could make a decision, Henry bounded over to me, dragging his arms half on the ground so that his movements resembled that of an ape. I drew in breath to scream—

—except all he did was sniff me. Like a Saint Bernard. First he sniffed at my crotch, then he did a shuffle around me and pressed his nose at the fabric of my Dockers right in line with my butt crack. "*Unnggh! Ungghh!*" he grunted.

"Mikey? Henry?" Fister entered the bathroom then. He saw us and halted. "Oh fuck me," he said, his voice completely inflectionless.

Victoria followed behind him only a moment later, heedless of the fact that this was a men's restroom. "Henry?" she said. She piled in right behind Fister and stopped. The bathroom was beginning to feel quite a bit crowded with the three of us and Henry inside.

For his part, Henry took advantage of their arrival to sniff them in much the same way. He sampled first Fister's crotch, then Victoria's. He might have worked his way around to the back end of either of them, but given the tight fit of the bathroom, they pressed themselves up against the sink and stared in horror down at Henry.

"Henry, oh my god!" Victoria cried. "What happened?"

"He's possessed," Fister said.

"Yeah, no shit he's possessed, Sherlock," Victoria said. "But how? Henry knows more arcane wards against demon possession than anyone."

I spotted Henry's iPhone lying discarded in the corner of the restroom. I bent over to pick it up, keeping my bunghole firmly angled away from Henry's invasive nose. It was a complex maneuver that surely looked more like a prison inmate trying not to be too obvious about picking up the soap, but thankfully Henry had stopped his examination of Fister and his mother and returned to the urinal to slurp at the urinal cake.

I thumbed the iPhone's button, and saw that Henry had left open a website—Wikipedia—in his web browser. I quickly scanned the site, and it confirmed my suspicions. "He summoned it on purpose," I told Fister and Victoria.

Victoria stared at me, stricken, then looked to her son. "Henry, why?" she said. As if he would divert his attention from the lollipop of the urinal cake and answer her.

"Feraphilia Olfacterosum," I read off of Henry's iPhone screen. "It's a sniffer demon. He must have invited it to possess him—"

"—so we could track Cherry!" Fister said. "That's brilliant!"

I snapped my fingers. "Of course! We still have Cherry's G-string in the back seat of the car. Do you think . . . could he follow her scent?"

"Yes!" Fister said. "Morpheus, you're a genius."

"No!" Victoria countered. "Give me the phone. I want to see that website. We're getting that demon out of him right now. What's the exorcism rite?"

"Um—" I pinched to enlarge the text on the iPhone screen, then squinted at the information on Wikipedia. "Looks like . . . cinnamon."

"That's it?" Victoria said. "Cinnamon?"

"Well, that and . . . eeewww."

"What is it?" Victoria demanded.

"You don't really want to know."

"Give me that." Victoria wrenched the iPhone out of my hands. She stared down at the screen. A moment later, she grimaced. "Eeewww." She handed me back the iPhone and looked down at Henry. "As soon as we find this demon, you are so grounded, young man."

I examined the phone again. "He sent us a text message," I said. "Or rather," I looked to Victoria, "he sent you a text message."

Victoria patted the pockets of her trench coat, looking for her cell phone. "I left my phone in the club. Shit!"

"What'd he say?" Fister asked.

I held the phone up to the light and read Henry's message:

"He's right," Fister said. "It just might work. It's not like we have any better ideas."

Victoria visibly wrestled with indecision for a moment. Finally, she sighed. "All right. You—" She pointed to Fister. "—go to the kitchen and convince them to give you as much cinnamon as you can get. You—" She pointed to me. "You'd better go out to the car and get Cherry's panties."

CHAPTER THREE

We hurriedly paid for our food, which we weren't going to be able to eat. We used the excuse that we were doctors and we'd gotten an emergency call—which was at least partially true. Fister took about ten point four seconds to wrangle the hostess into giving him a shaker of cinnamon from the kitchen; all it took was for him to flash his dimples and spout some sort of pseudo-medical jargon-loaded bullshit about the curative effects of cinnamon—"You could help us save a life," he'd said—and the young lady gave it over to him with a batting of her eyes and a starstruck look. I recognized it as the same trick Fister had used in high school to cozen the cheerleaders out of their panties.

Then, we piled back into Victoria's Azera, in the same configuration as when we'd left Jerry McTitties'—which meant I was relegated to the back seat once again, with Henry. We were barely underway before he went down on me, burying his nose in my lap and sniffing at my crotch. "*Mmmm, mnnngh,*" he grunted. And then, he muttered a word that might have been "Smegma", but fortunately his diction was muffled in the zipper of my Dockers.

"Here," I gently but firmly lifted Henry's head out of my crotch, interrupting him in mid-reach for my fly. I distracted him with Cherry's G-string that he'd lifted back at the gentlemen's club. He snatched the postage-stamp sized piece of lingerie out of my hands and brought it up to his nose. He inhaled deeply, and a beatific smile lit up his face.

"Can you understand me?" I said to him. "Can you follow this scent?"

Fister, in the driver's seat, obliged him by hitting the switch to roll down Henry's window. Henry—or the sniffer demon inside him—seemed to understand. Or rather, the aroma of demon-tainted snatch from Cherry's lingerie was alluring enough for him to cooperate, I imagined. Either way, Henry obligingly stuck his head out the window like a Saint Bernard on a road trip, and sniffed. He sampled the scents on the breeze, and then pointed off to the east. And he actually woofed—like a dog. Either that, or he might have been saying, "Muff! Muff!"—I couldn't tell which. I wasn't exactly much of an expert on the vocabulary of Feraphilia Olfacterosum demons, and I preferred not to speculate.

"I'm on it!" Fister said. He pulled a one-eighty across three lanes of traffic and sped off in the direction Henry had indicated.

Fister drove without any consideration for speed limits—or safety. I buckled up my seatbelt, just in case, and fretted constantly for Henry, who couldn't exactly do the same. He had to remain as he was, with his head hanging out the window and tongue lolling. Unfortunately, his butt was angled toward me inside the vehicle, and the ridiculous furry little tail on his honey badger costume kept alternating between brushing against my arm and wagging against my face. I weathered this for a few minutes before I couldn't take it any longer. I took advantage of Henry's demon possession: I reached out and ripped the tail off, ripping a butt-sized chunk out of the seat of the honey badger costume in the process.

At least Henry was wearing boxers. I heaved a mental sigh of relief for that small favor.

Fortunately, the Feraphilia Olfacterosum inhabiting Henry seemed completely unconcerned about the condition of the clothing of its human vessel. I took advantage of this and rolled down my own window and chucked Henry's tail out the window onto the highway. I didn't know if Henry would have any memory of what had happened during his possession when we eventually vanquished the demon inside him. I hoped not. Because if he did, I had a hunch that just for once, Honey Badger really would give a fuck.

Fister kept an eye on Henry in the mirror on Victoria's side of the car, and Henry navigated by nose unerringly in the direction that Cherry had gone. It was a minor miracle that the scent still lingered in the air, given as far off the scent as we'd gotten, but then, demons shared a kinship. It appeared as if, to Henry, the scent of the demon was the most pungent ambrosia, and he led us constantly toward it. My own third eye yielded me nothing, but then, it had utterly failed in the club.

Until finally, as we drove by a Wal-Mart, Henry went crazy. He bounced up and down like an excited bloodhound, causing the back seat to reverberate, and started panting heavily. He bellowed something that I couldn't hear very well, since Henry's whole head was outside the car.

Apparently, Fister hadn't quite understood the demon's words, either. "What'd he say?" he asked. "Was it 'fuzz box?'"

Victoria, who was closer to Henry, shook her head. "No. I think it was 'fur burger.'"

"That must mean we're close," Fister concluded. He pulled into the Wal-Mart parking lot and began looking for a parking spot. "You don't think Cherry came here for a pint of Ben and Jerry's, do you?"

"We need to hurry," Victoria said. "If that demon in Cherry is hungry, there's no telling what kind of carnage it might cause."

Fister hadn't even finished parking the car when Henry bounded out of the car. Though the demon possessing him didn't appear to be the most articulate form of demon in the netherwordly bestiary, it knew enough to use Henry's hands to open the car door.

"Don't lose him!" Victoria cried. She deftly bounded out of the passenger side and sprinted off across the parking lot after Henry, not bothering to close her car door after her. Usually the one to bring up the rear, I was third this time. The momentary annoyance of unhitching my seat belt still put me in the chase ahead of Fister, who had to finish parking the car.

Victoria and I managed to keep about a half-dozen paces behind Henry. He disappeared from our sight for a second as he bounded inside the sliding doors. "Henry!" Victoria called, panicked.

We plowed inside on his tail. Fortunately, Henry had gotten distracted just inside the sliding doors by the female greeter, a blue-haired retiree, whose face was registering a near coronary-inducing shock as Henry's nose was buried in her crotch.

At least, given the diversion, we were able to catch up to Henry. "Henry!" Victoria called out. Unfortunately, Henry was utterly un-affected by her stern tone. Victoria could only flash the greeter a rueful grin, spread her hands, and say, "Sorry. He's—um—"

"He's autistic," I cut in. I hated to trivialize a serious and complicated psycho-social disorder in this fashion, but it was the only explanation I could come up with on the fly to explain away Henry's behavior.

Fortunately, Henry tired of the greeter's snatch quickly. At that moment he pulled himself up to his full height and sniffed the air. The yellow tint of the demon-infestation in his eyes seemed to blaze brighter as his face lit up with delight. He smiled cherubically, and bellowed, "*Queef! Queef!*" And then he was off across the store.

Fister had just barely caught up with us when we were on the move again, trailing Henry. He led us past the cash wrap, through the racks in

Menswear, through the lingerie section, and then into an aisle that led past stationery toward the back of the store. There, his progress was arrested by a lady in a mobility scooter who was parked blocking the entire aisle, seemingly oblivious to us behind her. She was talking to her white-trash teenage daughter, who looked to be about sixteen, who wore a black tank top, painted-on eyebrows, a nose ring, and an apparently permanent scowl.

Henry was not to be deterred, however. "*Queef! Queef!*" he bellowed at the top of his lungs.

That got their attention. The woman and the girl both looked at Henry. "What did you say?" the woman demanded.

Henry fidgeted his frustration at being unable to get by them. He looked like a dog on a leash trying to chase a squirrel. "*Queef! Queef!*" Henry bellowed out again. He sniffed the air. "Yum!"

The old woman in the mobility scooter narrowed her eyes. "What a rude little child." She fixed Victoria and me with her glare. "You need to teach your kid some manners."

Victoria and I both started talking at once. Victoria pasted on a placating smile. "Oh, no, you see, he's not talking about you—" Victoria said.

"He's not my kid," I said.

The woman's teenaged daughter joined in the fray. "Oh no you didn't," she said. "Oh, hell no! My mama can't help it if—"

"I'll handle this," Fister said, pushing his way in front of Victoria and me. "Look," he said, "your vaginal flatulence is not really our concern. You see, we really just want—"

Henry interrupted him. He sniffed the air again, and reoriented on his quarry. "*Queef! Queef!*" He barked, and hotfooted it back the direction we'd just come.

"—to take you two beautiful ladies' picture. . ." Fister said. He brought his iPhone up and snapped a photo of the scowling pair. ". . . for *People of Wal-Mart dot com*. Have a nice day."

We bolted off across the store again, this time heading past office supplies and angling through housewares. Fister paused just long enough to pluck a pair of plungers off a bottom rack. "Here." He tossed one to me.

Great, I thought. *Just what I always wanted: going into battle with a demon armed with a plunger.*

Henry's madcap sprint across the store took him whizzing past about a dozen midnight customers, all of whom gave us scowls or withering stares. One burly man wearing a too-short white T-shirt, blue jeans, and a burgeoning case of plumber's crack even shouted after us, "Hey, assholes! Control your fucking kid!"

Henry finally came to a halt in the laundry detergent aisle. There was only one woman there: a blonde bombshell with a rack that strained against her T-shirt that was about two sizes too small. She wasn't wearing a bra. When she saw Henry there, panting like a dog, she smiled. "Well hello there, little man," she said. And grinned.

Victoria came to stand behind Henry. She rested her hands protectively on his shoulders. "Cherry," she said by way of greeting. The icy tone of her voice left me no doubt that this was a prelude to a bitch-fight.

Cherry crossed her arms over her breasts—a move which disappointed me no end. "Vicky," she said. "I should have known."

"Vicky?" Fister said. "That's your stripper name? Not really all that original, is it—?"

Victoria withered him to silence with a glare. Then, she turned back to Cherry. "We can help you," she said. "We're . . . specialists. We banish demons all the time. We know you've got one . . . um . . . inside you."

Cherry laughed derisively. "I'm quite happy the way I am," she said. "Before it came into my life . . . I was weak."

"Yeah, I'll bet you were a real pussy," Fister put in.

I shook my head. "Not helping, Fisty," I muttered.

"Now," Cherry continued. And she shifted her stance so that her legs were open. "Behold."

She queefed. A long, flappy, gusty queef tinged with an underworldly rumble. I felt my eyes widen. There was no way an ordinary twat could produce that kind of queef.

"*Queef! Queef!*" Henry cried, delighted. Up to this point he'd been content to stand, somewhat restrained, during Victoria's and Cherry's posturing. But given what must have been an olfactory smorgasbord, he trotted forward, tongue lolling, toward Cherry.

"Henry, *no!*" Victoria cried.

Too late. Henry crossed the distance to Cherry. Given his demon-infested penchant for burying his nose in crotches, he was likely to come away with no nose at all.

Cherry spared him barely more than an annoyed glance. As he drew closer, she scissor-kicked into the air—

She wasn't wearing any underwear. Surprise.

—but her heels didn't connect with Henry's face. That had not been her intent. Instead, as Henry's face came into proximity of her crotch, she queefed again, this time only a brief puff, and a green cloud of gas spat out from between her legs, like an octopus inking a predator. The cloud caught Henry full in the face. He stopped in his tracks. His face registered shock.

And then he collapsed to the floor, unconscious.

"*Henry!*" Victoria shrieked. She glared at Cherry. "You bitch."

Cherry's lips spread in a smug grin. "Your son, I take it? I knew you were old, but I had no idea you were *that* old."

"If you hurt him I'll—"

"Let me take care of this." Fister pushed in front of me and Victoria, brandishing the plunger he'd plucked from housewares in his right hand. He stepped over Henry's unconscious body and closed in on Cherry like a trained fencer, complete with upraised left arm for counterbalance. By way of a hilt he held it just above the rubber part.

"Fisty, no!" I called. But then, why would Fister choose now to start listening to me? He feinted and thrust. Cherry was ready for his attack. In a move only a stripper could pull off, she planted her back against the shelf of laundry detergent, reached over her head for the shelf above, and used it as leverage to swing her legs up into the air. They scissored out—

The demon hybrid inhabiting the moist domain between Cherry's legs caught the tip of Fister's plunger. For a second Fister and Cherry both struggled with the plunger. And then there was a large *snapping* sound. Fister stumbled backward. When he caught his balance again, he stared wide-eyed at the snapped-off end of his plunger.

"Fisty, you dumbass!" I shouted. "Wrong end."

Cherry smirked. "I bet you get that a lot, don't you, loverboy?"

Fister at least heeded me this time. He shifted his grip on the plunger and assumed his fencing stance once again, this time menacing Cherry with the rubber plunger end. He pressed his attack quickly. "*Yaaaaaaghhhhh!*" he bellowed, and closed in on Cherry.

"Fisty, watch out!" I cried. "Her . . . her . . ."

Damn. I still couldn't bring myself to shout out *vagina* in a public place. I hoped Fisty wouldn't pay for my odd little hangup.

Cherry met his thrust with a counter-move of her own. She scissor-kicked in the air in a mirror of the move she'd performed on Henry, and another inky green cloud of vapor streamed from her nether parts.

Fister was ready for it, at least. At the last moment he turned his thrust into a feint. He spun on the balls of his heels, graceful as a ballerina, nimbly avoiding the debilitating cloud of vaj gas, and brought himself out of his pirouette just at the right moment to score a hit on Cherry. The rubber plunger end cupped Cherry's left boob . . .

"Ha!" Fister cried exultantly.

She filled out the rubber plunger quite well. Damn. That was one hell of a rack.

Everything stalled for a moment. Cherry stared down at the plunger cupping her boob, her expression one of only mild annoyance. Fister fixed his gaze on the plunger, too, and his expression was one of . . . disappointment. As if he'd been hoping for something much more dramatic.

Cherry hit him in the face with the flat of her palm. Taken completely by surprise, Fister stumbled backward. His grip on the plunger wobbled, but he didn't drop it. He stumbled backward a few steps, and might have barely managed to keep his balance—

—except he tripped over Henry's prone form still lying on the aisle floor. Fister crashed down next to Henry. The handle of the plunger snapped in two as he impacted with the ground.

"Fisty!" I cried.

Cherry swaggered the few steps to stand over Fister. She straddled his body, and then sneered down at him. "Nice try, lover," she said. And then she began to lower herself down on her haunches to teabag his face.

I could only watch and listen in horror as the horrible ruffling queefy sound built again—

—but at the last moment, Fister managed to heave the rubber end of the plunger on its jagged remnants of a stick up. It caught Cherry full between the legs. The demon-powered queef flapped out into the head of the plunger, which also trapped the noxious, inky vaj fumes.

Cherry's smirk turned to a look of utter shock. She slowly lowered her gaze to contemplate her own midriff. Gagging and coughing echoed from the cavern between her legs, muffled by the erstwhile plug of the plunger, as the demon hybrid inhabiting her nether regions inhaled its own toxic fumes. Then, Cherry's entire body spasmed once, twice, and keeled over backward.

Fister managed to wriggle out just in time to avoid Cherry collapsing fully on top of him. He stumbled his way back to his feet and stared down at Cherry's prone form. "How do you like that, you smelly cunt?" he muttered.

With the melee over, Victoria and I raced down the aisle toward Fister. While Victoria knelt down over Henry, I clapped Fister on the shoulder. "You did it," I said. "Nice work, Fisty."

Fisty grinned like a schoolboy. "It was nothing," he said. "I just—"

He broke off. He perked his ears to listen to something. I did, too, and I followed the sound:

Queefing.

I gazed down to the end of the aisle behind where Victoria and I had come from. A half-dozen women in black hooker mini-skirts stood there in a line, completely cutting off the end of the aisle.

My dread suspicion was confirmed a moment later as I swiveled my head to look down toward the end of the aisle in the other direction. There, another half-dozen mini-skirted damsels cut off any possibility of a retreat.

"It's a trap!" I said. The Admiral-Ackbar rasp in my voice was dead-on, though completely unintentional.

At either end of the aisle, the hooker-like beauties kicked their legs into the air in perfect synchronization like demonic Rockettes. They were the perfect picture of balance.

The fluffy sound of queefing filled the air. It was the last thing I heard before I inhaled the noxious, slightly yeasty odor of week-old fishy smelling vaginas—

And I knew no more.

CHAPTER FOUR

Even though my throbbing head rebelled against the idea, I opened my eyes. I groaned. Prismatic light shone in my eyes, and I blinked at the sudden luminosity. Only after several seconds of blinking did I manage to squint my eyesight into focus.

A woman with a halo was staring down at me. No—not a halo, I realized a moment later. That was just the light filtering in through the window behind her. Which meant it must be morning. I'd been out for at least eight hours, then.

The woman drew nearer. She was wearing a habit, and a wimple—a nun. And judging by effigy of Christ I could just barely make out behind her, I must be in a church. Except I wasn't in much of a position to observe my surroundings. I was lying on my back—

—and as the feeling returned to my limbs and I tried to stir, I realized I was tied down. My wrists were shackled to clamps set into the floor, and my ankles similarly bound. I was splayed out like a crucified fish on land; all I could do was flop around ineffectually against my bonds. I wasn't going anywhere.

And I was naked. Oddly enough, I realized this about two point three seconds before the chill of a stone floor on my bare-ass backside reached my brain. It was backward, I know, but the tip-off was the nun's gaze: her eyes focused on my midriff. I instinctively bucked and thrashed against my shackles. I mean, I was buck-naked splayed out in front of a nun. I had an overwhelming impulse to shield my privates.

"They're waking up." The nun's voice was feminine, though sepulchral—demon-tinged. I frowned. I'd heard demons speak plenty of times before . . .

. . . but then, this nun's mouth hadn't moved. It wasn't her mouth that was speaking.

"Mikey?" It was Fister's voice. He was right next to me. I glanced to my left, and saw that he was similarly restrained, perhaps a foot and a half away from me. Just beyond him was Henry. And they were just as naked as I was. Victoria was nowhere to be seen.

The nun withdrew. I felt marginally better, though still I had to fight against the utterly unscratchable itch to shield my privates. I forced myself not to struggle against my bonds. "Fisty," I said. "Are you all right?"

Fister groaned. "I've got one motherfuck of a headache."

"Yeah. Me, too." Henry joined the conversation.

"Henry?" I asked. "You're back?"

"Yeah," he grunted. "I think so." There was a clink of metal as he apparently tried to struggle against his bonds as well. He eventually seemed to realize it was futile, and relaxed. After a moment of silence, he said, "My pubes really itch."

"So that's why you smell like cinnamon," Fister said. "Well, at least the nuns sent the Feraphilia Olfacterosum back for us."

"You're welcome," a demonic-tinged voice said. I struggled to tilt my head to get a view of the speaker, though I needn't have bothered. A second later Fister, Henry, and I were staring up at an unholy trinity of naked nuns standing over our faces. In the morning light filtering into where-the-hell-ever we were, I could make out rings of razor-sharp, serrated teeth ringing the bearded snatch of the one standing over me. I shuddered with revulsion at the sight.

Fister apparently found his wayward religion. "Oh, dear Lord in Heaven!" he exclaimed.

And Henry, ever graceful under pressure, waited a beat, then chimed in with, "You know, this should be way cooler."

I knew what he meant. Nothing like a prime wet dream scenario turned into a horrible nightmare by a ring of teeth.

"Welcome, demon hunters," the snatch in my line of sight said. I watched with morbid fascination as the lips contracted and contorted, like a real mouth. Given my nun's lack of landscaping, it was like watching Grizzly Adams with teeth.

It was Henry who conjured his mock-bravado first. "What have you done with my mother? If you've hurt her I'll—"

The trinity of twats laughed. "Don't worry, little man," the one standing over Henry said. "Your mother is fine. She'll make a fine vessel. If you're a good little boy, we'll even let you see her before you die."

Henry's bravado evaporated. "Um—no, thanks. That's all right," he said. "I'm good."

"What are you?" Fister cut in. "How many of you are there?"

The twats laughed in unison again. "More than you could possibly imagine." Fister's had a vaguely Jersey accent. *More* came out like *moah*. I frowned. What the hell kind of demon had a Jersey accent?

But then, these weren't demons, exactly. My demonic Spidey sense didn't react to them like it did to normal, run-of-the-mill demons. They were demonic in nature, surely—I mean, *Christ*, it didn't take a rocket scientist to figure that out. "You were spawned here, on this plane, weren't you?" I butted into the conversation. "You're completely terrestrial in origin."

The one above my face hissed. The nun squatted down lower, and I got a bird's-eye view of the creature. I grimaced and scrunched closed my eyes—which didn't help much. The creature's breath had a distinctly fishy odor. "Very perceptive," the creature hissed. "We are more alike than you could imagine. You might have been able to join us . . . if you had the right equipment."

"Sorry," I muttered. "I rather like my . . . equipment."

The three weird sisters tittered, an unsettling guffaw of laughter. "So will she," the one hovering dangerously near my face said. "So will she."

"'She?'" I said. "Who is 'she?'"

"Our Holy Mother," the Jersey-accented one over Fister said. *Mother* came out *mudder*.

"I take it you're not referring to the Virgin Mary?" I said.

They only laughed, that same, eerily synchronized laugh that launched shivers up and down my spine. "You'll meet her soon enough," the one over me said. "Until then, save your strength, demon hunters." They tittered again, and then they all squatted lower, and gas-queefed us into oblivion.

I groaned awake again. This time, opening my eyes made little difference in what I could see: it was completely dark. I'd been unconscious all the way through till nighttime.

"Nice of you to join us, Mikey," Fister's voice said next to me.

I didn't bother lolling my head over to see if I could look at him. My head was still swimming in a funk of crotch-musk. It still lingered in my nostrils.

"How long have you been awake?" I asked him.

"'Bout ten minutes, give or take," Fister answered.

"And Henry?"

"I'm here," Henry's reedy voice answered in the darkness.

"I see." I searched for something to say, but the lingering twatty smell pre-empted my thoughts. I sneezed. And then I sneezed again.

"I know how you feel," Fister said. "I think I'm gonna go strictly gay. I don't think I can ever look at a vagina the same way again."

"No kidding," Henry chimed in. "I think I'm scarred for life."

"Sorry, champ," I said.

"Yeah," Fister echoed. "Really, really sorry. The first vagina to come that close to sitting on your face should be a magical experience, not . . . well, *that*."

"No worries," Henry said. "I probably won't live long enough to need therapy anyway."

"That's the spirit, champ," Fister said. "Hakuna matata."

We lay there in silence for a moment. "It's worse than we imagined," I said at length. "We thought we were chasing one demon. Looks like there's a whole army of them. And more on the way." I wondered if Victoria had already gone over to the enemy. If she had, that would definitely put paid to all my late-night fantasies of ever getting in her pants.

"We need to think of a way to get out of these handcuffs," Fister said. He considered for a moment. Then, he inclined his head over to address Henry. "You don't happen to be double-jointed in your wrist, do you? I know Mikey's not. If he were, he'd have a way better sex life."

"Afraid not," Henry said.

There was a brief silence. Finally, I said, "Well, what do we know about these demons? We may not have access to Wikipedia, but there must be something. Some weakness we could exploit. Every demon has a weakness, right?"

"We could maybe pee all over them the next time they come in," Henry suggested.

"You think they're susceptible to urine?"

"Doubt it. But what other weapon do we have?"

"Hmm," Fister said. "Right now I'm leaning a little left. I'm afraid all I could manage to do like this is pee all over my own leg."

"That's easily fixed," I said. "It doesn't take much to give you a hard-on."

"Well, that's great in theory," Fister said. "But we have no idea if—or when—those nuns are gonna come back. I can't just manufacture a hard-on with a moment's notice. You gotta romance these things." He paused. "But what about Henry?"

"What about me?" Henry said.

"You're thirteen. You're like a hard-on factory. Do you think you could—"

"Afraid not," Henry said. "I'm not really a . . . sticker-straighter-outer, if you know what I mean. In this position, I'm afraid the best I could do would be to piss in my own face."

"Not to mention that trying to piss through an erection isn't exactly the easiest thing in the world," I said. "No, I think peeing on the demons is out of the question."

"Well then," Fister said after a short pause. He rattled against his restraints in frustration. "I've got nothing."

"Yeah," I said. "Me, too."

We considered in silence. No ideas were forthcoming. Finally, Fister sighed. "Well, guys," he said, "I just want you to know that . . . that if this is really the end . . . I wouldn't have had it any other way. These last few months . . . fighting demons with you guys, and Victoria . . . it's been real."

"Shut up."

"No, I mean it. It's . . . we're the Psycho Proctologists. We made a great team."

"No, Fisty, I mean shut the fuck up. I think I hear something. Someone's coming."

My ears were vindicated a few heartbeats later. The door to whatever chamber we were in creaked open. I still couldn't see anything, but I knew we weren't alone. My heart *thumpa-thumpa*-ed in my chest. Was it the nuns, come back to begin their feast . . . to chew us into the afterlife?

Then, the sound of somebody tripping, and possibly stubbing their toe in the dark. "Fuck!" a familiar voice swore.

"Mom!" Henry called. "Mom, is that you?"

"Henry!"

"Mom, over here!"

Victoria shuffled along the stone floor. I sensed her as little more than a figure kneeling down over Henry two bodies to my left. "Henry!" she whispered. "Oh, Henry, thank God, are you all right?"

"I'm fine, mom. I'm just . . . *hey*!" Henry's voice rose several octaves on his yelp of surprise. "Watch it, mom, I'm . . . I'm naked."

"That's all right, bubby," Victoria said. "Don't worry. I can't really see anything anyway."

"Can you get us out of here?" Henry asked.

"I—I don't think so. Not yet, anyway. I'm not sure where these cunts keep the key."

"What about you?" I cut in. "Are you all right? I mean . . . they said . . ."

"Yeah," Victoria said, "I know. Believe me, they tried. Not a pretty story."

"But you're you. I mean . . . what happened? It didn't take?"

"I'll tell you later. They think I'm one of them, though. I'm playing along. I'm just waiting for the right moment to . . . well . . . to do . . . something," she concluded lamely.

"I'm filled with confidence," Fister put in. "So let me guess . . . you've got no plan whatsoever, right?"

"Well, not exactly. But I know they're going to move you somewhere. At dawn, I think. They're going to feed you to the mother creature."

"Yeah," I said. "We gathered that."

"So just hold tight," Victoria said. "I'll do what I can. Until then . . ."

"We're not really going anywhere," I said.

"Right." Victoria knelt down over Henry. I heard an audible smooch in the darkness. "Love you, kiddo."

"Mom! That's not my cheek!"

"Sorry. Just . . . don't give up hope. I'll be back. Just wait for my signal."

"What's the signal?" I asked. But Victoria didn't respond. She was already on her way back out of the chamber. She tripped over something and uttered a barely muffled *"Sonofamotherfuckingbitch!"*, and then was gone.

CHAPTER FIVE

Warm liquid splashing in my face brought me sputtering awake. My first instinct was to wipe the dripping water from my face, but my wrists chafed immediately against my bonds, so all I could manage was to blink uselessly.

I heard Fister's shriek of indignation directly to my left while my eyesight was still attempting to crystallize. "Ow, you bitch, you peed in my motherfucking eye! It burns! *It burns*!"

Fister was always quick to jump to conclusions—too quick, sometimes. I shook my head to clear the droplets out of my vision, and I licked my upper lip with my tongue. "It's water, Fisty," I said.

My visions—both my ordinary sight, and my demonic Spidey sense as well—finally came into focus. We were in the presence of a demon—one badass motherfucker of a demon, at that, because the tingling of my second sight was off the scales. It completely overwhelmed my terrestrial sight until I could take a deep breath to will away the demonic heebie-jeebies and access my normal senses.

We were upright this time, at least. Still chained—my wrists chained to the wall at my sides, and my ankles as well. But at least this time we weren't staring up at any toothy muff-monsters.

Instead, a woman stood before us. She looked ordinary, in a frumpy housewife sort of way: she was overweight by about a hundred pounds, which made her cheeks jowly like a dachshund. Her haircut was a bad shoulder-length approximation of a fashion model but tended more toward a bad bowl cut, which had the effect of making her look like a fat Amish lad. She was dressed in a flowing floral-print muumuu that ended at her beefy ankles.

Behind her was a score or so of similarly-attired women, most looking to be in their late thirties or forties. The nuns were nowhere to be seen. *Thank goodness for small favors*, I thought.

But what drew my gaze was behind them, even. A giant, gaping pit lay in the ground perhaps ten paces from the wall where Fister, Henry, and I were bound. It was ringed with teeth around the outside, making it a giant version of the twat creatures that had infested the nuns. *The Holy Mother*.

As I beheld it, the entire pit expanded, then contracted, as if it was breathing.

Fister had apparently taken in his surroundings at about the same speed as I had. "Great," he muttered. "I never thought I'd end up being fed to the Sarlaac."

"The what?" Henry said. "You know this demon?"

Fister shook his head. "Nah. Christ. Don't kids these days ever see any good movies?"

"I've never actually seen *The Lion King*," Henry admitted. "Before my time."

"Christ," Fister muttered. "The Sarlaac's not from *The Lion King*. If we make it out of here, we're gonna have to have a Netflix orgy."

At that moment, the lips on the giant, breathing pit fluttered, and the creature let out an enormous queef that rattled the foundations of our prison—which was some kind of giant empty warehouse, judging by the stark metal walls and the ceiling far, far above us. No telling where we were—if we were even in Compton any longer.

The stench hit us a moment later. It was like rotting trout mixed with roadkill and brimstone. I tried to keep from gagging. "Man, that's fucking foul!" Henry exclaimed. "What the hell has that thing been eating?"

The fat woman regarded Henry with a pert frown. "What a vulgar young man," she said disapprovingly. "But then, I expected as much. Like mother, like son."

"What about my mother?" Henry said. "What have you done with her? If you've hurt her, you bitch—"

The woman's mouth turned down in a lazy scowl. "She proved to be resistant to her companion. We've kept her for . . . reimplantation."

Henry spluttered a whole host of obscenities worthy of a sailor—and he *almost* managed to be more vulgar than his mother—but I paid him no heed. I narrowed my eyes at the woman. "You're Maggie," I said. "Aren't you? You knew Victoria back in college."

Fister looked askance at Maggie. "*You* used to be a stripper?" he said. "Man, you've let yourself go."

Maggie grimaced. "You try bearing five children and keeping your figure, asshole."

"Hey, look, I'm sorry," Fister said. "I know, I know, I'm a man, I'll never understand what it's like, but hey, I didn't cause your problems. Not all men are responsible for your problems. You didn't need to summon the biggest vajeej demon from the nether planes just to—"

Maggie shook her head. "Typical," she muttered. "That's so not what this is about."

Fister blinked. "It's not?"

"Of course not." She gestured to the gaping maw of the demon pit behind her. "The Holy Mother brings only purification."

"'Purification?'" Fister said. "What the fuck's so pure about that smelly twat?"

The entire row of women lined up behind Maggie hissed at Fister's insult, but she stayed them with a wave of her hand. Then, Maggie took a few steps forward to grasp Fister's chin. "I wouldn't expect you to understand," she said. "You're part of the problem. All of you. You're filthy."

"Hey," Fister said, "you're the one who peed on me, sweetheart. You're no fresh winter snow yourself."

Maggie scowled. "You see? Even now, in the face of purification, all you can do is make silly sex jokes." She spat out the word *sex* like it was cursed, and shuddered theatrically at the same time. Her entourage of muumuu-clad women behind her followed suit, doing a perfect imitation of her shudder. I wondered if the creatures that infested their snatches provided them with some kind of demonic telepathic link that allowed them to think and react as one, with Maggie as the spokesperson. "Toilet humor," she said, and grimaced.

"What other kind is there?" Fister said.

"Sex and debauchery are the hallmarks of a debased society," Maggie said. "It's everywhere . . . on TV . . . in the media . . . on *Ellen* . . . even in JC Penney ads."

"*Ellen* and JC Penney?" Fister said. "That's a bit random."

"It shall not be tolerated!" Maggie said, her voice pitching to a banshee-like screech. "There are still those of us who safeguard the morals of our civilization."

"Wait a minute," I said. "*Ellen* . . . JC Penney . . . something rings a bell . . ."

Maggie swelled with pride. "We are the custodians of decency and good Christian values, and our name will strike fear into the hearts of the perverse everywhere! We're—"

"Good Christian values?" Fister said. "You do know you're worshipping a giant cunt, right?"

Maggie ignored him. "We're the bane of immorality. We're one million moms, united in the cause of righteousness."

"One million moms?" Henry said. "There's only like twenty of you."

"Not for much longer," Maggie said. She gestured to the skanky pit behind her. "Soon . . . very soon . . ."

"Very soon what?" I prompted.

"She's pregnant," Maggie said, punctuating her statement with a Grinchy smile. "Any moment now she'll launch her spores into the world, and every woman on Earth will be our companion."

I tried to follow the line of her boasting in my head. My eyes widened. "You . . . you can't be serious."

"Oh yes," Maggie said. "Our holy mother has enough spores in her right now to infest every woman on the planet."

"You're bluffing."

Maggie shrugged. "You'll never find out, though, will you? Your bones will give her the nourishment she needs to spawn. You'll be too dead to see the new world order."

New world order. I did the math. "But . . . if one of those things takes up residence in every . . . every . . ."

"Vagina, Mikey," Fister put in. "Christ, just say it for once, will ya?"

"In every vagina in the world . . ."

"Then nobody's ever gonna have sex again," Henry concluded.

"Except for anal sex," Fister pointed out. "And gay sex. Can't take those away from us, can you, bitch?"

Maggie shrugged. "That is the responsibility of our brethren."

Fister's smug expression faded. "What? Brethren? You have brethren? That's so cheating."

"Why destroy sex for everyone on the entire planet?" Fister asked. "I mean, yeesh, just 'cause your hoo-hah closed up shop years ago—"

"So that we can start over," Maggie said. "Think of it: a glorious new world order, freed of the preoccupations of the flesh—"

"A world full of blue balls?" Fister said. "You don't think making sex lethal is gonna stop people from thinking about it, do you?"

"The memory of it will soon fade into the footnotes of human history," Maggie said.

"So will humanity itself," I said. "What's gonna happen if nobody can make babies? We'll go extinct within a hundred years."

"The Holy Mother's offspring will continue to be fruitful," Maggie said. "It has all been ordained."

"You mean those things in your snatches can procreate?" Fister said. He looked over to me. "That's . . . that's . . ."

"That's so gonna suck," Henry finished for him. "But hey, look on the bright side. At least we'll be dead."

As if in anticipation, the giant vaginal pit in the ground gave a burbly, belchy rumble. The lip-like folds of its walls agitated, as if sensing its meal. If it could have spoken, I imagined it would have said something like *Feed me, Seymour.*

The line of one million moms understood the command implicit in its rumbling: it was time. Maggie smiled beatifically. "Start with this one," she said, indicating Henry. "He's the unfortunate victim of poor parenting, but he's still young, and succulent. His suffering should be short. These, on the other hand," she continued, indicating Fister and me, "can reflect on their wicked ways while they watch their young friend die."

The entire throng of Maggie's henchwomen cackled with glee. They started chanting, and the four of them on the end swung off and approached Henry. One unlocked the shackles on his hands first at the same time as one released his legs while the other two restrained him. They may have been fat, but they were also strong—perhaps imbued with inhuman strength by the demonic hybrids hitchhiking in their twats. Henry thrashed and swore and struggled, but his efforts were in vain. They dragged him bodily toward the lip of the pit. The chanting rose in pitch and fervor. I closed my eyes so I wouldn't have to witness Henry's death throes as he was chomped and chewed by the gaping vaginal maw.

"Get your hands off my son, you cunts!"

I recognized that voice. It couldn't be—could it?

I opened my eyes. It was. My heart leaped with a thrill of hope as the chanting of the score or so of one million moms broke off.

Victoria stood perhaps twenty paces away from Maggie and the line of chanting women. Unfortunately, though, the army that I wished she had with her was nonexistent. She was alone. My short-lived hope crashed and burned. Dumbass bravado without much in the way of good sense to back it up was always going to be Victoria's undoing.

Maggie hissed. "You!" she said. "You were supposed to be back at the abbey, undergoing implantation."

"I was." Victoria shrugged. "It didn't take the second time, either."

"Impossible," Maggie spat.

"I'm a gynecologist," Victoria said. "I've been doing Kegel exercises for over a decade. Your 'companion' screamed as I strangled it to death."

Maggie's jaw clenched with fury. "This location is secret! How did you find us?"

"I just followed the smell," Victoria said. She swaggered a few steps closer. "So, Maggie, we meet again at last. It's been far too long." Victoria made a show of sizing up her adversary. "Damn, you've let yourself go."

Maggie didn't rise to the taunt. Instead, she responded with one of her own. "I've just been getting acquainted with your son," she said. "He's a thoroughly rotten little wretch . . . but I suppose that's to be expected given your pathetic excuse for parenting. A pity, really. He really is quite handsome . . . Chad's spitting image. I'll enjoy killing him, just like I did his father."

Henry blinked, confused. "'Chad?' My dad's name was Chad?" He looked to Maggie. "You killed my father?"

Victoria took Maggie's bait. She pulled a knife out of her boot and adopted a fighting stance. "Why don't you bring it, bitch?" Victoria said.

Maggie's mocking laughter echoed around the entire warehouse. "You came here by yourself?" she said. "Armed with only a knife? Brave, my dear, but foolish. You're hopelessly outnumbered."

"Maybe," Victoria said, "but I have this." Still brandishing the knife in her right hand, she plucked her cell phone out of her pocket with her left.

Maggie eyed the cell phone with disdain. "What are you gonna do with that? Even if you could get ahold of somebody before we kill you, they'll never believe you."

"I have friends," Victoria said.

Maggie bleated with derisive laughter. "Now I know you're bluffing, my dear. I know full well you've got only two friends in the world," she hooked a thumb at Fister and me, "and they're not in any position to come to your aid."

My stomach churned: it was the feeling of my last hope in the world being backed over by a tank. I knew Maggie was right. Victoria wasn't much of a social animal. Henry, Fister, and me—the Psycho Proctologists—*were* her social circle.

"Oh yeah?" Victoria taunted. "Joke's on you, bitch." She held the cell phone up to her ear and said one word into it: "*Now.*"

Nothing happened. A protracted moment of silence hung over the entire warehouse.

Eventually, Maggie and her entire line of harpies tittered with laughter.

Victoria stared balefully at the phone. She shook it once with her hand. "Fuck!" she swore. "No service? You've gotta be kidding me. Fuck T-Mobile!"

Maggie turned to the four acolytes who were still holding onto Henry. "Throw him in the pit," she ordered.

"No!" Victoria screamed.

Victoria's appearance, as ultimately fuck-all worthless as it had been, had accomplished one thing. She'd stalled for time. Henry's handlers had relaxed their grip just enough on him. He kicked one on the left in the shin, and with the resultant shift in grip he managed to administer the same kick on the one to his right. The two tubbies screeched in pain and collapsed, and the opening enabled Henry to break free. He pivoted, and caught one of the women unawares. With a vicious shove to her back, he sent her stumbling forward, where she collided with her comrade. Both of them tumbled into the Holy Mother, who received the unexpected meal with a satisfied gurgling sound.

Inwardly, I cheered on Henry and Victoria, but the pessimistic part of my brain still couldn't help thinking that the odds were still nineteen against two. Fister and I weren't in much of a position to lend a hand.

But Henry, fortunately, was no dummy. He feinted running toward his mother—predictably. He waited until Maggie commanded her minions, "Get him! I'll take care of this bitch!", and when the line of flab-packers waddled into motion to intercept him, he veered off his trajectory and broke straight for Fister and me.

His diversion bought him enough time to fumble at Fister's shackles. "Nice work, kiddo," he said to Henry. "You got the key off them."

"What can I say?" Henry beamed. "I've got magic fingers. Remind me to thank Janice McSweeney for letting me practice on her bra."

He managed to get Fister's hands freed, and then he set to work releasing Fister's ankles. But then time ran out. The leader of the line of stampeding cows, somewhat lighter and nimbler than the rest, closed in on him, bellowing like an enraged rhino.

"Keep working!" Fister said. "I got this."

He met the woman's charge. With the benefit of his hands free, he swung the manacle on the chain and connected solidly with one of the woman's chins. She grunted, and her eyes rolled up in her head.

"Got it!" Henry said.

And Fister was free. He took a few awkward steps as the feeling returned to his ankles. He looked down at Henry. "You free Mikey," he said. "I'll lead them off."

And Fister, as good as his word, howled with berserker fury and charged the advancing line of harpies. Unarmed, with not a stitch of clothing, he somehow managed to muster enough sound and fury with enough conviction to give the line pause, like Han Solo charging an entire line of stormtroopers on the Death Star. It was enough time for Henry to pop the manacles on my left hand.

I watched as Fister's fierce bravado petered out on him. He came near the collision point with the line, and—no fool, he—he veered off just in time, cruising in an arc around the lip of the gaping vagina creature pit. The line of bitches hesitated, just for a second. No geniuses there—much to my relief. They blinked in unison, and then veered off after Fister, leaving Henry the time he needed to pop off my bonds. He managed to release the manacles around my right wrist. Now with both hands free, I rubbed my wrist with the thumb and middle finger of my other hand to try to jump-start the circulation.

"He's sure brave," Henry said.

"Yeah," I said. "Cross your fingers and hope he doesn't lose a finger like Bob did. Or worse." If those bitches managed to tackle and pin Fister— and across the distance separating us, I saw that they were dangerously close on his tail—he'd suddenly find himself not half the man he used to be.

While Henry worried at the bonds on my ankles, I flicked my gaze about twenty paces to the left to see how Victoria was faring. She and Maggie were duking it out on the fringes of the Holy Mother. Maggie had Victoria backed up, teetering on the edge, and as I watched Maggie landed a solid upper cut square on Victoria's jaw. Victoria reeled, teetered—

I clamped down hard on my instinct to call out. There was absolutely nothing I could do to help her, and if I distracted Henry from his task, he'd likely go sprinting off across the warehouse to take on Maggie himself, which would ultimately avail us nothing.

Fortunately, Victoria was a fighter. She wobbled a bit, her arms flailing, then finally regained her balance just in time to keep from plunging into the pit. She even managed to recover with enough panache to taunt Maggie with a *come on, bitch, is that all you've got* gesture. Infuriated, Maggie roared and kicked up high into the air. Thankfully, her stripper pole days were well behind her; she wasn't anywhere near as flexible as Cherry, nor as leggy, and the weaponized ink cloud she queefed in Victoria's direction hovered about chest-high. Victoria's face would have been well clear of it, except Victoria had seized her opportunity to tuck and roll under Maggie's upthrust leg—

—directly into the cloud of musk.

Victoria's deftly executed tuck and roll, designed to put herself behind Maggie, out of the lip of the Holy Mother, disintegrated into a graceless belly-flop, like a somersault performed by a retarded three-year old.

"Come on, Victoria, get up," I muttered. Had she taken a full load of Maggie's crotch ammo, or just a glancing blow? From my angle, I couldn't quite tell.

At that moment, Henry keyed open the last of my bonds. I took a hesitant step, my sleep-prickled ankles threatening to buckle under my weight, but by the barest grace I managed to remain on my feet.

"Go!" I told Henry. "Go help your mother. I'll help Fister."

Henry wasted no time. He turned, and seeing his mother sprawled out, insensate, with Maggie straddling her, he erupted with a roar of fury fit to match Fister's, and bolted off across the warehouse floor. His roar was enough to distract Maggie from lowering herself onto Victoria's face and chewing the coup-de-grâce, at least.

It'd have to be enough. Fister had problems of his own. The nineteen remaining acolytes of the Holy Mother weren't much in the brains department, but it didn't take much to leverage tactics when they had Fister outnumbered nineteen to one. They had him surrounded in a tightening circle of spring-colored muumuus.

My turn. Fister's and Henry's tactics seemed to be sound, so I followed their lead and hollered and whooped at the top of my lungs and charged toward Fister.

Except apparently, I sounded more fearsome in my own mind than I did in real life. My bellow of challenge went completely unrecognized. The circle continued squeezing in on Fister, heedless of me. Such was my disappointment that my bravado actually dissipated, and my mad charge petered out.

Shit. Time for plan B. I had no weapons, and at best two point three seconds before Fister disappeared under the smear-the-queer pile of fanged cunts.

"Mikey!" Fister called out to me plaintively. "Help me!"

There was nothing else I could do. I burst into motion again, foregoing the berserker roar that I couldn't quite sell with enough conviction, and charged. It turned out to be a blessing in disguise that none of the twats paid any attention to me. I closed in in their numbers. "Fisty, get down!" I called out, hoping he could hear me over the sound of the gnashing teeth in his general vicinity.

I plowed into the circle from behind. It was like hitting the sweet spot in a rack of bowling pins. The heifers all went flying, their flabby legs and arms twining and tangling in an inextricable clusterfuck of limbs.

Fister had heard me. He rolled out from underneath the mess, came to a halt on the cold stone floor of the warehouse, and grinned up at me.

"Fisty!" I reached out a hand to help him to his feet. He lithely hopped up.

"Nice timing, Mikey!" he said.

We embraced. It was totally a bro-motivated hug, like tight ends after scoring the winning touchdown in the endzone, but we both realized that, given the fact that we weren't wearing any clothes, it seemed just a tad . . . gay. So we both cleared our throats in unison and stepped apart, and opted to finish our celebration with a lame high-five instead.

A chorus of shrieks of rage and pain and fury derailed the moment anyway. We turned, and beheld the pile of cunts. The jigsaw puzzle of arms and legs splayed in every which direction was more intricately intertwined than the raunchiest lesbian scissoring orgy porn.

And the demon hybrids between each of those women's legs were hungry—and indiscriminate about their meals. I grimaced as the wet sounds of chomping and chewing mingled with the shrieks of pain and shock of the creatures' hosts. I averted my eyes from the scene of carnage, but Fister glanced directly at the pile of indiscriminate munchers. He shuddered. "Damn," he said. "Those skanky things will eat anything."

There was little time to spare for them. I shifted my attention across the warehouse, to the last spot where I'd seen Victoria battling Maggie, to see how she'd fared while Fister and I had been otherwise occupied—

—and my breath caught in my throat. Victoria was lying on the ground, dazed, only a few feet away from where Maggie had Henry in a chokehold at the edge of the pit that housed the Holy Mother. Her arms were clamped around his neck, slowly throttling him. Henry could only put up feeble, ineffectual struggles against Maggie's superhuman strength. The Holy Mother trembled in anticipation of her meal, and emitted a skanky queef that rattled the entire floor of the warehouse.

"Henry!" I shouted. "Hang on!"

I started to run toward him, followed closely by Fister, but I stopped maybe about ten paces away as Maggie spared a demonic, leering glance in our direction. "Stay back, demon hunters," she warned. "If you come any closer, I'll kill him."

While Fister helped Victoria to her feet, I held up my hands in a placating gesture to Maggie, like I was a negotiator trying to defuse a hostage situation. "Your minions are all gone," I told Maggie. "If you harm him, there'll be nothing to stop the rest of us from killing you. It's finished, Maggie."

Maggie bared her teeth at me. "I would gladly give my life to usher in the reign of the Holy Mother," she said.

I considered. "Prove it," I called her bluff. "Go ahead and jump in."

"Mikey—" Fister said, "I'm not sure that's such a good—"

I ignored him. "Go on," I urged Maggie. "It's simple. All you've gotta do is jump over the edge. You can take Henry with you, and you win."

Maggie grinned. "I prefer the alternative."

"What alternative?" I said. "We seem to be at an impasse."

Maggie spared Henry a contemplative glance. "It really is a pity," she said. "He's a pretty lad. He could have lived in the brave new world, completely free of corrupting influences." She glared across at Victoria, who, with Fister's help, limped up to my side. "But he's *ruined*." She spat out this last word. "He's a filthy, vulgar little shit. So much like his father."

"My . . . father?" Henry managed to croak out despite Maggie's clamphold on his neck. "Who . . . who was he?" He looked across the distance separating him from his mother. He and Victoria locked gazes. I could see the utter confusion in Henry's eyes.

"You've never told him about his father?" Maggie said. "Oh, Victoria, for shame, why not?

He's your son. He deserves to know the truth. Why don't you tell him now? Why don't you tell him what a filthy, disgusting pervert his father was?"

Victoria glared across at Maggie. "His father was a good man," she said. "He was a little kinky, but so what? I loved that about him."

"You should have seen how he leered at me. How he pawed at me. Right before I killed him."

Victoria started toward Maggie. I intercepted her and physically had to restrain her from tearing across the distance separating her from Maggie. If Victoria hadn't been injured, I likely never would have been able to stop her. "Don't," I warned. "If you force her hand, Henry will die."

"But—"

Anything Victoria might have said was cut off at that moment by the throes of the Holy Mother. Her lips flagellated spasmodically, and an abominable smell, like that of rotting corpses, wafted up from her nethers to assault our nostrils. Fister, Victoria, and I all recoiled at the stench.

And then, a single, fur-covered ball of teeth launched up out of the pit of the Holy Mother. Fister, Victoria, and I could only watch as it arced high up into the air, nearly grazing the warehouse ceiling high above us, then plopped onto the warehouse floor about ten paces from where Victoria was standing. It lay dazed for a moment, and then jittered to life. It spun around a few times, like a compass searching for north, and then oriented on Victoria. It began scooting across the floor toward her.

"Ah." Maggie grinned. "The sporing has begun. You're too late."

I felt my eyes widen. I imagined millions of those furry little tribble-like monstrosities with teeth geysering out of the Holy Mother, all of them seeking out warm, furry, moist places in the women of the world in which to roost.

And I realized that Maggie had been stalling us. Waiting until the ultimate trump card played itself. And like idiots, we'd been content to sit here yapping while the Holy Mother came closer and closer to germinating.

Maggie's cackling, exultant laughter echoed throughout the entire warehouse. "You've lost!" she cried. "Rejoice, for the new world order is nigh!"

A crashing din drowned out any further peals of Maggie's laughter. At first I thought it was the Holy Mother, but then, that didn't make sense. The Holy Mother's queefing discharge was an organic sound, and this one was metallic, jarring, grating—

It was behind me. I turned around to see the entire back wall of the warehouse disintegrate into rubble as big-rig oil tanker plowed through it at full throttle. Fister, Victoria, and I all instinctively crouched down and tucked into a triangle, hanging our heads in together to keep from being hit by flying debris.

The oil tanker screeched to a halt only mere feet from where we crouched. Victoria, Fister, and I slowly uncrouched and straightened.

"What is this?" Maggie cried.

I ignored her. Instead, I looked to the cab of the oil tanker. The driver's side door of the cab opened, and a figure hopped out onto the concrete warehouse floor.

It was Bob. He looked over to Victoria and grinned. "Somebody order an oil tanker?" he said.

Victoria grinned. "Bob, you're a sight for sore eyes. Though I think this may be the first time anybody's ever said this to you: it sure took you long enough to come."

"Nice try!" Maggie screeched. "But you're too late! Nothing can stop the coming of the Holy Mother now."

But the distraction of the oil tanker's arrival must have slackened her grip. "Put a fucking sock in it, you fat fucking cunt," Henry said. He lashed out with his foot, and landed a solid blow on Maggie's knee. It buckled, and she collapsed under her own weight with a howl of pain and fury. Without wasting any time, Henry pivoted, whirled, and kicked Maggie squarely in the face. She fell over backward, directly into the pit of the Holy Mother, who received her with a gleeful flurry of chomping followed by a satisfied queef.

As Maggie's screams died away, Victoria raced across the distance separating her. "Henry!" she cried. She wrapped her son in a furious hug, and he returned it, for once not protesting that he was naked.

Bob came forward to stand next to Fister and me. We were still a safe distance from the edge of the Holy Mother's pit. From there, Bob craned his neck to consider the creature from the pit. "Damn," he muttered. "That is one nasty fucking cunt."

"Understatement of the year," Fister muttered.

"That's the thing that took my finger?" he said. He held up the shortened middle finger of his maimed hand and flipped off the Holy Mother. "Take that, you bitch."

As if in answer, the Holy Mother's lips writhed again, and another furry tooth-creature arced out.

Victoria cut short her celebration with Henry. She sprinted back to where the rest of us were standing, trailing Henry. "Come on, Bob. We don't have much time. One more thing to do."

She led Bob back to the oil tanker. Under her direction, he climbed back up into the cab, put the rig in neutral, and nudged the accelerator. The giant semi tanker inched forward. He jumped down out of the cab just before it plunged into the gaping maw of the Holy Mother, followed directly after by the rest of the oil tanker. The Holy Mother stretched to receive it, like being penetrated by an enormous steel dildo . . .

And as we watched, the entire rig disappeared into her gaping maw.

And then she began to chew. I clamped my hands over my ears at the horrific sounds of her fangs rending and shredding the steel of the tanker. Apparently, the Holy Mother really would eat just about anything. I shuddered: I'd come within a hair's breadth of being a meal for her.

Bob reached into his pocket. He pulled out a book of matches, lit one, winked at all of us. "Y'all had better run," he said. And then, he chucked the match into the gaping pit of the Holy Mother.

We ran. Fister, Victoria, Henry, and I hotfooted it out of the warehouse, across the strew of concrete rubble that sliced at our bare feet, but we barely noticed. We didn't stop until we were out of the warehouse, into the sun of a new morning.

Bob followed only a few seconds after us. He bolted out into the open air, his flannelled belly jiggling from side to side.

We were all thrown to the ground by the roaring explosion as the entire warehouse went up in a ginormous fireball. It rose into the air, and the resultant shockwave pelted us with a blast of heat.

We slowly got back to our feet and stared at the ruin of the warehouse. "We did it," Victoria said. Henry came to stand by her side, and she ruffled his hair affectionately. "We did it, kiddo."

"Yeah." Henry grinned. "We did it."

EPILOGUE

Three days later, we celebrated surviving our latest brush with death by popping Henry's *Lion King* cherry. The kid knew perhaps more than any other human being alive about demons, but the gaps in his cinematic lexicon were gaping. One of these days, we'd pop his original *Star Wars* trilogy cherry, but for the moment, given the freshness of the memories of the Holy Mother, it was too soon to subject the poor kid—and me—to the battle at the Sarlaac pit. I hoped that the next time I sat down to watch *Return of the Jedi*, I could do so without having horrible flashbacks to the smelly, cavernous maw of the Holy Mother.

After watching the movie at my place, we were all hungry, so we all piled into Victoria's Azera. Strangely enough, she tossed her keys to Fister. "You drive," she said. Then, she looked to me. "You ride up front."

"Me?" I blinked. I never got to ride up front.

"Yeah, you." Victoria smiled. "I wanna talk to my son."

And so we rode that way. While Fister drove and I enjoyed the ride in silence, Victoria and Henry had their conversation via text messages in the back seat. It was odd, hearing the rapid fire alerts from their phones, but I understood that it gave them a measure of privacy to have their much-needed mother-son conversation. I guessed that the thrust of the conversation was about Henry's father. Victoria was finally ready to open up to him about it.

The drive stretched out. Eventually, I understood where Fister was taking us. When we passed by Jerry McTitties', all lit up in neon-y splendor for the weekend crowd, Fister slowed. "Isn't it beautiful?" he said.

"Beautiful?" I said. "It's a seedy strip club, Fisty."

"Yeah, but think about the sex," Fister said. "Right now, every guy in that place has a hard-on, and they're all thinking about sex. They're all fantasizing about banging those strippers in there, and ya know what's so amazing about all that?"

Had I known Fister for far too long, that I could pick up on his logic so easily? "No teeth?" I said.

"Exactly," Fister said. "Think about all the people everywhere around the world who are screwing right now, or about to screw, or just got finished screwing. They can nail each other all they want. Because of us. We saved sex for the entire world."

"And nobody will ever know," I mused.

"It doesn't matter. We know."

And that would have to do. There was still the business of the mysterious "brethren" Maggie had referred to.   Her brethren were out there somewhere, and I was sure they'd rear their ugly heads sometime . . . probably soon. But until then, victory was ours.

"There's still one more thing left to do," Fister said.

"What's that?"

"You'll see." He executed a few more turns, and finally turned into the parking lot at the Denny's where we'd stopped three nights earlier on the hunt for Cherry. "Who's hungry?"

We went inside. The hostess made to seat us in the far corner this time, but the table where we'd sat three nights ago was open, so we requested to sit there. The hostess obliged, and we settled in. I had an odd case of déjà vu, but at least this time there were no demons on the loose. I was relaxed, and contented. No worries.

In the far corner, a pair of young lovers fed each other bites of blueberry waffles and smooched in between. They were young, and in love. I thought they'd probably fuck each other later tonight. *You're welcome*, I thought, and smiled.

The waitress came over and took our orders. Fister ordered last, and after he finished ordering his giant stack of pancakes and the waitress wandered away, he reached inside his jacket pocket and set a shaker of cinnamon on the table. "This belongs back in the kitchen," he said. "I promised I'd return it."

I grinned and shook my head. "You drove us all the way out here to Compton to return a shaker of cinnamon?" I said.

"Well, not just that."

"Then what?"

"I came here for you, Mikey."

"Me? I don't understand."

"So you can practice."

"Huh? Practice what?"

"Come on. You can say it. You know you want to."

I frowned. "Say what?"

"You know. *Vagina*."

I grimaced. "Will you keep your voice down? This is a public place."

"Exactly. Come on, Mikey. Let 'er rip. You can say it out loud, I know it. Vagina!"

I cast a surreptitious look around the restaurant. There were a handful of other patrons. So far, none of them had overheard Fister.

Victoria and Henry laughed. "He's right, Mikey," Henry said. "Come on. You can do it. Just repeat after me: *Vagina!*"

"I don't—"

Even Victoria joined in. "It's all right," she said. "Try it. Vagina!"

"*Vagina!*" Fister cried louder.

"*Vagina!*" Henry echoed.

We had the attention of the entire restaurant now. The two lovers were looking at us, perplexed, but many of the other patrons were scowling openly at us, obviously displeased that three grown adults could be so vulgar in the presence of a thirteen-year-old kid.

What the hell? I thought. There would always be crazy cunts like Maggie in this world who thought they knew best what kids should be exposed to and what they shouldn't. Who thought that you could keep your kids innocent forever by sheltering them from everything the world had to offer . . . especially sex.

Well, they could fuck themselves.

Why not? *No worries*, I thought. Feeling emboldened, I stood. Thanks to Fister's and Henry's and Victoria's prelude, I had the eyes of everyone in the restaurant on me. I grinned broadly, and then, at the top of my lungs, I bellowed, "VAAAAAAGIIIIIINNAAAAAA!"

Hakuna matata, motherfuckers.

AUTHOR'S AFTERWARD

My dearest sick fucks,

If you've read this far, then I congratulate you. You truly are one of the few, the proud . . . one of the unique few who could stand up in a crowded Denny's and yell, *"Vagina!"* (Yeah, I dare you. I triple dog dare you. If you do, make sure to make a video and send it to me at

psychoproctologists@hotmail.com .

You can send me any other compliments or kudos at the same address.

If you're a concerned parent who'd like to flame me for spawning the Psycho Proctologists, I'd love to hear from you, too.

You can also visit my YouTube channel, where you can see homemade book trailers:

www.youtube.com/psychoproctologists

Or on Facebook:

www.facebook.com/psychoproctologists

Or drop by the Psycho Proctologists blog and leave a comment:

www.psychoproctologists.blogspot.com

Sincerely,

W.W. Pecker

Read on for a preview of

Psycho Proctologists

and the Urethrae
of
Annihilation

The third volume in the epic *Psycho Proctologists series*

by

W.W. Pecker

"Hmm," Victoria said, frowning down at my crotch. "Funny, Mikey, I'd have pegged you for a boxers kind of guy."

I stared stupidly at her for several seconds. I blinked once, twice, trying to clear the fuzz of sleep from my brain. I'd just crawled out of bed less than two minutes ago . . . what the hell was Victoria doing in my house? Why was she standing over my stove with a spatula in her hand and bacon sizzling in a frying pan on the burner?

Not that she was an unwelcome sight by any means. She was wearing a pair of my sweatpants and a white T-shirt, and by the way the morning light shone in through the half-slatted picture windows I could tell she wasn't wearing a bra. The outline of one nipple underneath the flimsy T-shirt in her profile poked me in the eye from across the room.

Seemingly oblivious to my scrutiny, she nodded at my crotch. "Please tell me you have a bathrobe. You'll put somebody's eye out with that thing if you don't watch out."

I shook my head to clear it of the sleep fuzz. I grew aware of two things simultaneously: my state of undress . . .

. . . that, and my morning wood standing at attention inside my underwear.

At that moment Henry skidded into the room from the back hallway that led off toward my guest bedroom. He caught sight of me and immediately shielded his eyes with the back of his hand. "Whoa, Doc M! Dude . . . I mean . . . damn, dude."

I tried to shield myself by cupping my hands in front of my crotch—rather vainly, unfortunately. With the raging tent in my underwear, there was not really anywhere I could place my hands so as to hide my tumescence. I experimented with a couple of different configurations , and when I realized I was failing miserably I settled for strategically backing down the hallway that led toward my bedroom. "Wha—what are you two doing in my house?" I said. "What the—"

My undignified retreat was cut off a moment later as I backed into Fister. He'd padded up the hallway toward me, and in my state of absorption at finding Victoria and Henry both in their pajamas in my condo at six thirty in the morning, I'd failed to register his presence. But as I bumped into him, I yelped and turned around, and then when I realized in so doing I was flashing my ass-cheeks to both Henry and Victoria in the kitchen, I whirled around again.

"Mikey, a thong? Really?" Fister shook his head and chuckled. "I guess we all wanna feel pretty when we go to bed, huh?" He shuffled around me in the tight corridor, and as he passed me gave me a playful slap on my left ass-cheek. "Morning, tiger," he said. And then he shuffled into the kitchen to join Henry and Victoria.

I opened my mouth to demand an explanation, then closed it again, and opted instead to salvage what little remained of my dignity. I retreated back into my bedroom, all the way into the bathroom. There, I fumbled to put the lid down on the toilet. In my still sleep-befuddled flusterment, the lid banged down with a deafening crash. I didn't care. I sat my thong-bared ass cheeks down on the toilet and forced myself to take deep breaths.

What the fuck? What the motherfucking fuckety fuck? I wracked my memory to try to find some reason why the entire gang would be in my condo like pre-teens at a sleepover. I hadn't invited them, I was fairly certain of that. Had I?

The sleep-addlement faded far, far quicker than my morning wood. Under other circumstances, I might have spanked the problem into submission, but with Fister and Henry and Victoria—*damn*, those breasts!—only footsteps away out in my kitchen, I couldn't exactly take the matter into my hands so directly, even though the sight of Victoria's perky little nipple through her flimsy T-shirt begged for such a solution—

So not helping, I thought. Forcefully, I tried to clear my mind. I wished then that I'd taken Fister up on the Buddhist meditation classes that he'd signed up for on a lark about six months ago, because trying to get the sight of Victoria's delights out of my memory was like trying to put a jack-in-the-box back in the box after it had already sprung.

So I did the next best thing. I whipped off my underwear and climbed into my shower. I cranked it on—cold—and hopped in. I huddled in the corner and waited for my morning chubby to disappear.

And waited.

Finally, though, when my teeth were chattering from the chill of the water on my bare skin, I achieved control of my body. And since there's nothing worse than a cold shower in the morning, I quickly cranked the water to hot. I stayed in long enough for the chill to leave my body, then I got out, dried off, and peeked my head out into my bedroom.

The coast was clear here, at least. I expected my bedroom to have been invaded during the interim of my shower, but fortunately, I was able to rummage unmolested in my clothes drawers for something to wear.

Only when I was dressed in my baggiest pair of jeans did I head back out to the kitchen. By that time, Fister, Victoria, and Henry were all seated around the table in my breakfast nook enjoying a fine breakfast. They looked for all the world like a normal family sitting down to a casual breakfast—except they weren't my family . . .

I took the fourth seat around my square table. A quick round of surreptitious gazes and furtive glances made a circuit and a half around the table. Nobody seemed to want to make eye contact with me, and for my part, I couldn't quite look any of them in the eye, either.

Fortunately, Henry broke the silence first. "Here, Doc," he said, passing me a plate loaded with crispy strips of bacon and sausages. "Mom makes a mean breakfast." The hints of a sly grin spread at the corners of his mouth. "The sausage is especially . . . thick."

Victoria missed nary a beat in reaching over and slapping him on the back of the head even as he snickered at his own innuendo. At the same time, she glared at Fister across the table from her, and he obligingly aborted his own echoing snicker. With effort, he summoned a straight face, though he only managed to keep it by hunching lower over his plate of fried eggs and focusing intently on breaking the yolks with his fork.

The sausages really did look amazing, and I realized that I was famished. So I helped myself to four slices of bacon, three sausage links, then wordlessly accepted the small plate of fried eggs and fried potatoes that Victoria passed to me. Then, I reached across the table and grabbed the last two remaining slices of toast from a plate there.

I was halfway through buttering my toast before I managed to say, feigning nonchalance, as if I were merely inquiring about the weather, "Sooooo . . . you wanna tell me what the hell you're all doing in my house?"

They all three traded glances, as if silently drawing straws. Henry lost. "You mean you don't remember?" he said.

"I think I'd remember if I'd invited you over to stay the night," I said. "Not that I would do such a thing on a Wednesday." I glanced over at Henry. "On a school day," I added pointedly. "Please don't tell me . . .there's not . . . I mean, you haven't . . . it's not . . ."

"Of course it is," Henry said. "What else would it be?"

Demons, I thought, and shivered. Things had been so quiet after we'd defeated the Holy Mother and foiled her plot to booby-trap sex for the giant mass of heterosexual men everywhere. I'd actually almost been lulled into believing that I could lead a normal life again.

Almost . . .

"I got an IM from one of Morpheus's online contacts last night about ten o'clock," Henry continued, "that indicated you might be in danger. So we all drove over here to check on you. When we got here, you were already asleep, so we just . . . let ourselves in."

"In danger?" I said. "Me? What . . . why me? I mean . . . just me? Not the rest of you?"

Henry spread his hands. "What can I say? Demons work in mysterious ways. I'm afraid that's about all I know at the moment."

"But don't worry," Victoria put in. "We'll follow up on it today. We'll get it sorted."

"You don't think . . . maybe . . . should I stay home today?" I absently took a bite of sausage. "I mean, if I'm in danger—"

"I doubt any demons will try anything in broad daylight," Fister said. "Nah, don't let on like you suspect anything. You should go to work like normal. I mean, there's all kinds of D-listers who need their buttholes examined."

I inwardly breathed a sigh of relief. I had an appointment for a follow-up consultation on Pat Robertson's anismus today, and it would be a total bitch to reschedule. Not to mention Donny Osmond's rectal prolapse . . .

"All right," I said, "but is there anything I can do? "I've got a hole in my schedule at eleven."

Fuck. I could tell by all three of their unison grins that I'd set them up perfectly without even realizing it. Normally, I'd have paid more attention than that. But they'd all caught me by surprise this morning . . .

"You're a proctologist, Mikey." By some unspoken accord, Victoria drew the privilege of delivering the zinger: "Isn't that all you've got is holes in your schedule?"

After I got over the initial shock of having the comfortable bubble of my morning routine penetrated and punctured, I was actually kind of touched by my friends' concern. After all, they'd dropped everything they were doing last night and come driving over to my house with the only thought on their minds being my safety—if you overlooked the breaking and entering, of course.

Either that, a pernicious, nagging voice in the back part of my brain cut in, *or they were just out of groceries and knew your fridge would be stocked.*

It was an uncharitable thought, though, and I banished it. I arrived at my clinic in a rather chipper mood. I greeted Elian and Dolores, my hyper-efficient front office staff, and threw myself into my day with vigor. *Bring on the bungholes*, I thought, and grinned.

"You have nothing to worry about, Mr. Robertson," I found myself reassuring Pat Robertson just slightly before eleven o'clock as I walked him personally back to the waiting room. I tried to walk all my patients back to the waiting room after their treatments or consultations—except Kirk Cameron, of course, who I usually just left alone in waiting room three to rub one out with all my implements. I'd gotten that little practice from my dad, who always used to say it was the little things like that that showed your patients they were more than just assholes to you. "In fact," I continued, "I'm confident that you'll be back to regular bowel movements again before you can say 'hallelujah.'"

His face tried to smile, I think. It looked more like a botox-impeded twitch, unfortunately. In person and up close, without the benefit of his coterie of makeup artists and stylists, he looked like refried death. In fact, I had to stifle a kamikaze giggle as I imagined him in a black robe and hunching over a scythe. He'd be a dead ringer for the grim reaper—except . . . slouchier.

"Good news, doc," he said. "Praise—"

I cut him off. "Just keep following the exercise regimen I prescribed, and I'm sure you'll feel full of shit again in no time."

"That's . . . such a relief. At my age—"

"Oh, pish." I grinned my most effervescent grin and made a gesture as if to swat his concern away. "I'm sure you've got plenty of shit still left in you, you old devil you."

I waved him on out of the waiting room with a handful of further platitudes, then turned to find Dolores frowning over the tops of her half-framed spectacles at me. She raised an eyebrow archly. "What's gotten into you today, doc?" she asked.

"What? Too much?" I said. "You don't think he caught on, do you?"

"That senile old coot? Oh, hell, no. They don't come much more oblivious than that."

"Then what is it?" I asked. "Not funny? I've been saving up my best material all week just for him."

"No, that was a pretty good one, doc."

"Then what?"

"I don't know. You're feeling kind of . . . spunky today." She narrowed her eyes. "Did you get laid last night?"

"Oh. My. God!" Elian shuffled up, punctuating every word. Elian was a consummate professional with patients, but every once in a while, when the waiting room was empty like this, his drag queen alter ego, Ms. Perky Marilyn LeDoux, which he performed onstage Wednesday nights at the Coxbury, shone through. "Doctor M, you didn't!" He thumped me playfully on the middle of my chest with the backs of his fingertips. "I didn't know you were seeing anyone."

I feigned offense. "What makes you think I'm seeing someone?" I said. "Maybe I had a one-night stand."

Elian and Dolores both exchanged a look. Then, in unison, they both looked back at me, and Dolores spoke for the both of them: "Yeah, right."

"I could have," I said defensively. "I mean, I'm a doctor. Chicks totally dig that."

"Mmmm-hhmmm," Dolores said. She shot Elian a look, and together they returned to typing at their computers.

Elian and Dolores had both been with my practice for years, and they were great at their jobs, but sometimes . . . sometimes I just wished for office staff that didn't treat me as if I were an open book. A particularly boring open book, at that. I wondered if Bruce Wayne ever felt like this. At least he was smart enough to have a butler who knew how totally badass he really was.

Oh, well. I'd just have to content myself with knowing that I'd saved the world from the ravages of demons—twice now. Hell, it was only because Fisty, Henry, Victoria and I had taken out the Holy Mother about a month ago that people could still have one-night stands.

"Well . . . we don't have any appointments till afternoon," I said. "I'm going to go take a nap in examination room two. 'Cause . . . you know . . . it was a long night last night. Of totally wild sex."

"Whatever you say, doc," Dolores said, still typing away at her computer.

I retreated to examination room two. There, I obsessive-compulsively straightened the white paper covering on the examination table. I wasn't really tired, though, so I sat in my office chair in the corner. I crossed my legs and stared at the medical model of the rectum on the table beside me. I should be using this time to catch up on paperwork, but instead I pulled out my iPhone. I opened up the calendar app and examined my schedule. It had all my appointments, of course, not to mention my Toastmasters meeting for tomorrow evening. Everything perfectly laid out and organized.

I pulled up Friday. There, from seven o'clock in the evening, I'd scheduled MOVIE NIGHT, just as I had every Friday night for the past three months. This month's offering was *The River Wild*, because I was making my way systematically through the oeuvre of Kevin Bacon. On a whim, I erased MOVIE NIGHT and typed in instead: ONE-NIGHT STAND. Maybe it was finally time to go try speed-dating like Fister was always encouraging me to do. According to Fisty, all I had to do was say I was a doctor— which was utterly true—and it was an instant poon magnet to the over-thirty single women crowd. An M.D. was even better than a bubble butt or a six-pack or even a killer pair of dimples when it came to single women my age who were feeling the inexorable passage of time and the siren lure of security and stability.

I imagined walking into the basement of the Presbyterian Church, smiling confidently around at all the singles and knowing that I could have my pick of the litter that night. Maybe I'd find some curvaceous redhead with a perky bust and a killer smile . . .

Fuck. My imagination—the one in my head, that is—had unwittingly conjured an image of Victoria. And the imagination that resided in my pants responded in kind. And unknowingly I'd already sailed past the point of no return where trying to shut off the processional of mental images was nigh impossible.

Oh well. I knew well enough where this ship would need to put into port. I reached over and locked the door to the examination room, then pulled down my pants, freeing my . . . imagination.

And was it just my imagination, or was everything down there just a little bit . . . *more* than usual? Maybe it was just the kind of day I was having, but all the colors of my world seemed just a little bit brighter. The veins just a little bit veinier purple, the knob just a bit more swollen red . . .

My imagination conjured a vision of Victoria as Fräulein Maria in The Sound of Music running through the Alps singing "The hills are alive . . ."— because that was the best visual I could come up with when life seemed just a little bit too technocolor for reality—except instead of a nun's habit Victoria was wearing the T-shirt she'd been wearing as she stood over my stove this morning, displaying underneath a maddening little hint of . . .

Three short, sharp buzzes in quick succession brought the sound of music in my imagination to a screeching halt. *Shit! Mother of Jesus H. freaking*

Christ shit! It was my office staff's signal for emergency. Usually it meant Fister. I thanked my lucky stars I'd remembered to lock the door.

But instead, a second later, Henry's voice came piping through the intercom to me. "Doctor M, Doctor M, we've got a medical emergency out here. You'd better come right away. Justin Bieber is here. He sprained his sphincter trying to pull another fifteen minutes of fame out of his ass."

Henry? What the ever-loving fuck was he doing here? With a groan, I pulled up my pants, tucking myself gingerly into my work khakis, made sure to fasten my white lab coat around my midriff, and exited examination room two.

I found Henry in the waiting room, alone with Dolores and Elian. Dolores had a rather unrestrained look of annoyance on her face. She hated kids, which is why she'd gotten out of a pediatric office faster than a spray of explosive diarrhea. Elian looked highly bemused. "Ah, Doc," he said, "you've got a. . . em . . . friend here to visit you."

The questions I had for Henry tumbled over themselves in their haste to be uttered. "Henry? What are you doing here? How did you get here? Shouldn't you be in school?" Holmes Middle was a long way from here . . .

Henry shrugged. "I never actually went to school today. What the hell . . . it's just the standardized testing window, anyway. I took the bus here. It wasn't far. I never actually went home after waking up at your place this morning."

Both Dolores and Elian buried their heads in their computer screens, but I caught their sideways glances at this bit of information, and I replayed in my head the entire tongue-in-cheek conversation I'd just had with them not ten minutes ago about the one-night stand I'd had last night. I opened my mouth to stammer some kind of explanation. "I—I—"

"So this is your office, huh?" Henry said, casting an interested look around. "Cool. Can I see the examination rooms? Do you have those . . . those . . . hell, I don't know what they're called . . . those legs-up things like my mother has?"

"Stirrups," I said. "They're called . . . no, I don't have stirrups."

"Mmm," Henry said. "Too bad."

"Henry . . . what the hell are you doing here?"

He cocked his head in a very poorly disguised nod at Elian and Dolores, a motion that said as plain as day: *not in front of the muggles.*

"Right," I said, and took a deep breath. "Why don't you go on back into examination room two? I'll be right behind you."

Henry did as he was bid. In his wake, I turned to Elian and Dolores. "He's . . . he's . . . he's such a pain in the ass, really. He's my nephew."

Dolores arched an eyebrow at me. "You don't say, doc," she said. "You never mentioned you had a sibling."

Fuck, I thought. She had me there. I pulled my hands out of the pockets of my lab coat and spread them helplessly.

Which was even worse, because Dolores's attention went immediately to the bulge in my pants, and her eyes went round.

"I—" I stammered. Finally, I gave up trying to fish for an explanation and slinked off back to examination room two. There, I found Henry staring in fascination at the plastic medical model of the rectum.   "What is it, Henry, that's so urgent?" I demanded.

"We need to go," Henry said.

"Go? Go where?"

"To rescue Fister and my mom.   They're in trouble."